TRICK

GODDESS   TY

eBook ISBN   978-0-9992784-9-9
Print ISBN   978-0-9992784-6-8

Dedication

This part ended up being the hardest part to write -- not because there were so many people I wanted to dedicate this book to -- but quite the opposite. It is that the few people who kept encouraging me to write, who believed in me, my crafts and wanted the best for me who constantly motivated me and stood behind every dream or idea I have ever had made it hard to find the words to express my love and gratitude. It is seldom, especially nowadays, that you come across people that genuinely applaud and encourage your successes as much as their own without some deep internal ulterior motive or spite. Thank each and everyone of you for your support and advice. I would also like to dedicate and acknowledge the two young gentlemen who approved me using their likeness in my book. I reached out and they helped, and it's greatly appreciated #ITHWH.

A special thanks to my publisher and editor for assisting me on this journey and help making it possible.

Chapter One

Sitting here listening to Foolish by Ashanti, feeling precisely that -- FOOLISH -- as I sip my wine and scroll up and down multiple social media apps trying my best not to fall asleep. *'It's one a.m. ONE IN THE FUCKING MORNING,'* I angrily thought to myself. All I wanted was a simple night at home with him; a candlelit dinner, deep intellectual conversation, and of course some wild, earth-shattering, passionate sex that would put my ancestors to shame.

'I'm over it,' I thought as I got up to blow out the candles that were strategically placed around the apartment. I turned off the speakers bellowing out all the jams to my, yet again, broken heart. I barely make it to the bed, tipsy and tumbling. I lay flat on my back staring into the darkness questioning myself and why I choose to stay with a person who neither values nor adds value to my existence. My thoughts shortly interrupted by the sounds of footsteps and doors opening and closing.

"Baby," he calls. I don't answer, I lay there quietly and motionless pretending to be asleep. "Baby," he calls again in his deep masculine tone, sounding closer than before. Yet again I ignore him, but I can feel him crawling into bed, up between my legs and planting kisses from leg to leg until he reaches my knees. "Baby," he calls yet again, and yet again, I ignore him. He resumes kissing upward until he has made it to my freshly shaven pussy. '*Fuck,*' was all I could think as each kiss made me wetter and wetter with anticipation. "Baby, wake up," he whispered.

"Hmm," I moaned answering him fake sleepily. Guess that's all he needed, he placed a small sweet kiss on my pussy lips, spread them with two fingers and slowly began to lick my clitoris as my body jerked from the reaction. "Mmmm," I moaned. Cupping my titties through the black satin nightgown with lace trim, I rubbed my pierced nipples as he started making circular motions with his tongue and introduced a finger to play. I don't know what it is, but something about him was different tonight, maybe he knew he really fucked up and felt bad but whatever it was this was a new side to him. As if one finger wasn't enough, he slid another deep into my vagina. I gasped.

"Awww FUCK," I moaned out in ecstasy as he rubbed his thumb against my asshole gently poking still sucking on my clitoris. My body was slightly shaking as I came on his fingers. Pulling his head closer to me and biting the sheets, I tried to keep myself from screaming at the top of my lungs.

5

ring, ring

At this point, I'm aching for the dick. I mean, I knew whatever time he made it in that I would give it to him, but the way he was serving me this head... although fully satisfied from it, I almost feel like he deserves it despite being late.

ring, ring

I push his head from between my legs and motion for him to come to me. He kisses up my stomach as he continues fingering me, making his way up -- even flicking my navel ring with his tongue -- until he reaches my titty and starts licking and sucking on my nipple. He grabs hold of my double D cup, massaging my breast as he takes a mouthful. He puts the two fingers from my vagina into my mouth. "Mmmm," I moan attempting to reach his dick and put it in after feeling its hardened thickness throbbing against my pussy.

ring, ring

"HELLO!" I answer angrily.

"Girl, I know your ass is not still in the bed." My cousin Ciara, or Ci-Ci, snaps back.

"What?!" I was confused as all hell as to why she's calling blowing up my phone and interrupting quite possibly the best apology sex I have ever had. "Just call me once you get yourself together, don't you have a full schedule today? Does brunch with me at eleven ring a bell?" She asks, sounding irritated. I sat up, checked the time on the phone and instantly rolled my eyes. Nine A. M. I looked around and noticed no one else was here. "Yeah, I'll call you back or see you at the brunch spot," I responded. She followed up with an okay, and we both hung up.

A dream. A fucking dream. Of course, that would explain why everything was damn near perfect. Sex between us wasn't nowhere near as good anymore -- somewhere along the lines, he had turned into a selfish lover. The kind of lover that was more concerned with getting himself off and uncaring to the satisfaction of their partner; the kind that gets their rocks off and rolls over, leaving you to have to finish yourself off and wonder whether it was even worth it. You know, the kind that makes you question why you even allowed him to enter your golden gates of mystique and euphoria for two minutes of pumping and anger that begs the question... does this even count as sex? I shower, get dressed, and do some much-needed hair maintenance which from the way I looked when I got up should've required a weed whacker and a rake. I finish up with my daily morning routine; brushing teeth, cleansing and moisturizing my face, putting on my scent of the day and the like. I called out to Siri asking her to schedule my Lyft as I attempted to straighten up the mess from last night. With a good ten minutes before the ride arrives, I applied some lip, grabbed my heels and handbag. As I make my way out of my apartment door, Siri chimes that my Lyft has arrived.

Thirty minutes later I finally arrive at Nellie's -- where I have been dying to attend the drag brunch for months. I picked up my cell to call Ci-Ci, "I'm here near the entrance." Knowing her, she's already here and two Mimosas in without me. "Finally," Ci-Ci says as she walks up to me. "Come on, we're over here," she directs me to our table. Ciara is this pretty, tall, feisty redbone with a smart mouth and heart of gold. She came dressed in an emerald green halter top, white high waisted ripped jeans, and open-toed white heels. "You look nice," I compliment her.

"You do too," she returned the sentiment. "You have the girls out, legs out, and heels on just showing off," she added. She wasn't wrong though, I haven't had much use for the styling and profiling as of late unless it involved me dolling up for the club. Most of my days were filled bouncing in and out of classes, having study sessions in the library with Ronni, and my nights at the strip club trying to save up funds for my own boutique. As of the last couple of months, things between John and I had been fizzling out, and I hadn't much energy to keep up with appearances for him. It wasn't like he gave a compliment or even acknowledged it. The only time I truly feel remotely sexy is when I'm doing bottle service, giving a lap dance when the men are playing grab ass with me, or the occasional nights when I am some older gentleman's arm candy for the night.

"So, what happened last night?" Ci-Ci asked.

"Nothing." I quickly responded then took a sip of my mimosa. I directed my attention to the entertainment as to avoid an embarrassing conversation.

"What do you mean NOTHING? I thought you had plans to have a night in with John to woo and seduce him in hopes to get that spark back in your relationship," she stated -- almost coarsely. I honestly didn't really feel like talking about it, I mean I did but not at that moment. I would have rathered watch as the young lady did her rendition of Beyoncé. I preferred to eat, drink and put him back to the furthest parts of my mind. I knew she wouldn't leave it alone, so I just gave her an answer. "Long story, short I had plans to have a night in with him, and he had other plans like always," I shrugged. Just as she started to ask more questions, the waiter comes over; he takes our orders, menus, and proceeds to his other tables.

ding

John: WYA??

Me: Why? What's up?

John: TF you mean why what's up?! WYA Moe?!

ME: OUT

John: Yea OK

"Are you okay?" Ci-Ci asked. I guess she sensed the frustrations or peeped the irritation in my face.

"Yeah, I am, why you ask?"

"Your whole mood just changed, and your face balled up looking really ugly," she said letting out an awkwardly uncomfortable chuckle.

"Yeah I'm good, that was just John asking where I am for whatever reason. Truth is, this was a long time coming and last night was the final straw. I can't keep watering a dead flower." She shook her head in agreeance. She never really cared much for him -- none of my friends did -- they all thought he was a one-sided, lazy, possessive, verbally abusive, manipulative asshole. I couldn't see it. Well... not at first anyway. Granted he was mean as hell, but he always seemed sweet on me up until we lost our baby. That's when he started drinking more, staying out, and using me as a punching bag for his verbal attacks. As unfortunate as it was, losing the baby it took a toll on the both of us. I saw it as a second chance to get my shit together, and he saw it as a death sentence, no longer giving a fuck about his life or anyone else in it. We spent all our time, energy and money back and forth to the hospitals, in legal fees, and burial costs. There was literally nothing more we could do and nothing that could bring him back. Slowly we began to silently hate each other, he more than I, obviously.

The more I seemed to heal, the more he appeared to hurt. He didn't want help -- not from me, his family, or a therapist. I didn't blame him for his anger, either. I was angry, too. At the world. At God. At everyone. Even myself. He was our first child. I carried him and loved him before I even knew who he was. I loved him before his little face could bless us with the first smile or his little hands tightly squeezed my finger as he cooed, but the backlash from John was becoming unbearable and toxic to my progression. "Hey, you still with me?" Ci-Ci asked as she snapped her fingers in my face.

"Huh?!" I responded puzzled.

"Thought I lost you there, I was telling you the food was here and looks and smells delicious and asking what exactly happened last night... you weren't exactly forthcoming with the details," she said. We sat there another twenty minutes enjoying the show, drinks, meals, and conversation. I amused her with my night and dream that she so rudely interrupted and she filled me in on her love interest, Mr. D, and about the bitches at her job who got her fucked up.

"Hey, look I have to run I need to get to the financial aid office, pay for my classes, and head to the apartment to get the money," I told Ci-Ci as I began gathering my things and paying the bill and tip.

"Oh, well I can drive you. We can make a whole day of it, I was just going to go shopping, and we can pop into the nail salon so you can do those things with me afterward."

She suggested excitedly, I smiled paid our bills and we waited as the valet brought her truck around. Once inside she connected her phone to the Bluetooth and immediately started playing tracks by Young Dolph, Gucci Mane, Black Youngsta, Moneybagg Yo, Kevin Gates and a few of our other favorite artists, including my favorite local, Lightshow. We were turning up to the music and twerking in our seats.

ring, ring

"Hello," I answered, Ci-Ci turned down the music, huffed, and gave me a mean side eye. "No, I haven't checked Blackboard for my final grades yet, but I feel hopeful plus you've been helping me a lot, so I'm sure I'm good. What about yourself?" I asked. "Okay, that's wonderful, congratulations. I'm about to check as soon as we get off the phone. I'm also on my way to the school to register for next semester, so I'll check in with you a little later to let you know how everything goes." Hanging up the phone, I attempted to turn back up the music.

"Hold up. Wait. Do you have a little school boo?" Ci-Ci asked real child-like.

"No, that was Ronni. We took a few courses together this semester, and she's been helping me so that I wouldn't fall behind." I laughed answering her finding it funny how she insinuated it being a boo.

"Why would you be falling behind?" She asked with seriousness. "You good? Are you okay?"

12

"I'm okay," I responded sitting up, adjusting in the seat. "It's just between classes, bills, and trying to save for the boutique, it's a lot especially without help and having to come back from the hole we were in after... uh..." My voice began to crack, tears formed in my eyes and my throat felt like it was tightening.

"It's okay." She said with one hand on the wheel and the other caressing my shoulder. "If you need help you can call me, with anything, you know that." She assured me.

"I know. I honestly don't know what I'm doing... I'm just trying to make it day by day." I said as I cleared my throat and caught the one tear that managed to escape my eye. I wasn't much of a crier -- not that I didn't do it or thought it was a sign of weakness, well slightly that -- but I just couldn't stand the idea of crying in front of people or displaying any sign of emotions.

"You are, and you're doing great... better than anyone that would have had to walk in your shoes. You're a queen. Don't forget that." She told me as she rubbed down the length of the wavy lace front I had installed before the weekend.

"Thank you," I managed with a chuckle not realizing we had stopped and was fully parked. Both of us got out of the truck and made our way to the building. "Go on ahead of me, you still have your spare key, right? I'm going to check the mail." She proceeded while I obtained the mail from the box. Bullshit, bullshit, bullshit, bill, bill... I was thinking to myself as I sifted through the envelopes.

"Bitch, what the fuck happened in here? Is this how you had this place and thought you were going to have a romantic night, last night?!" I could hear Ci-Ci talking to me from inside of the apartment just as I was making my way to the door. I stopped in my tracks. My mouth dropped and the envelopes I held started falling to the floor. I grasped for my purse to retrieve my phone.

"9-1-1, what's your emergency?" Asked the dispatch.

"I'd like to report a break in."

Chapter Two

A few months had passed since John broke into my apartment and took everything I had, well, everything I had of value anyway. He stole all the money I had stashed away for school and the boutique. Here I was, back in the club, rubbing elbows with Mr. Brown and having to start all over.

"Hey, baby girl. Mr. Brown really did miss your fine self." He expressed, whispering in my ear and placing his hand on the small of my back that was visible courtesy of my black, backless, mid-thigh length, form-fitting dress.

"I missed you too Mr. Brown." I lied as I placed one hand on his, then used the other to flag down the self-proclaimed third best bartender in D.C. (Me and the rest of his patrons knew that he was the absolute best.) Of course, I didn't miss Mr. Brown ass. He is a geriatric pervert with a bad case of erectile dysfunction. His nasty ass prayed on younger women for sexual favors in exchange for the bullshit they could get themselves if they went out for a job. I know, hypocritical, but I kept

15

him to myself to keep him away from them. If anything, I was saving them! Yeah right, who was I kidding? I needed the money too.

"What'll it be sweetheart?" The bartender asked in his low, soft, sensual voice that he used on his online radio show to talk the panties off women.

"I'll have a coke, no ice... and for my friend, a Pill Cosby," I answered, giving him a wink. I mouthed thank you once he returned with the drinks. I immediately turned my focus back to Mr. Brown, "here you go handsome." I gave him his drink, which he slowly sipped, then made the ugliest face imaginable like it was sour, and he got lock jawed.

"Woo baby girl, you trying to kill Mr. Brown before he gets to the goodies!" He exclaimed, glaring at me.

"Of course, not Mr. Brown that's just a little something to perk you up and make sure you keep up with me tonight." I lied, rolling my eyes in my head as I did often having to entertain bullshit with these people. "I have to go to the ladies' room to freshen up, I'll be right back." I lied again. I just wanted to slip away for a few minutes to give him time to get the drink down so by the time we left he could pass out and I'd lie about what an amazing night we had to keep him happy. He wasn't a bad looking old man though, I could tell in his younger days he may have had his way with women. He just wasn't my brand of old. I did have a penchant for older men though; something about a man with a little age, more wisdom, and decently established in life... I don't know... maybe I had some deep-rooted daddy issues I hadn't addressed, but something about the greying hair truly turned me on.

In the meantime, I decided to walk around, mix, mingle, and keep an eye out any new prospects for my client list -- mainly older gentleman who was more frivolous with their money and required less work to please. Someone who mainly just coveted the companionship of a young woman. Most I've come across didn't have wives or baby mothers they were stepping out on. Plus, my system was flawless; I had the bartender make the strongest drinks, tire them out on the dance floor, take them to a hotel, tell them what they want to hear, and tuck their old asses in goodnight. I'm already paid in advance for my time, so whether they get lucky is a gamble (and an added fee) for the most part. It doesn't get that far.

"SIN!" Rich, my manager, yelled at me.

"YES, BOSS!" I yelled back to him over the music, he motioned for me to follow him towards a back office. While walking back there, I happened to catch a reflection of him in one of the few dozen ceiling to floor mirrors that adorned the walls of the club. I noticed his biceps, triceps, pectoral muscles, and abs flexing from under his white tee shirt with some sort of crude sexual message about only liking women that enjoy giving blow jobs. I chuckled, thinking to myself 'are there any other kind of women in this world?'

He sat on the edge of the desk that was in the center of the room. I stood there in front of him, examining him. Noticing small details about him that I hadn't before. The tiny patch of grey in his neatly trimmed beard and small traces of it in the waves of his low cut. How decadently chocolate his skin was as it slightly glistened from whatever moisturizer he used under the fluorescent lighting in the office.

I slowly and seductively walked towards him, placing my knee on the top of the desk, standing over him, then started placing small sweet kisses on his lips and chin. I took his left hand and guided it up the back of my thigh until his hand was on my ass. With my other hand I grabbed the back of his head, still kissing him. He kissed back, inviting his tongue into my mouth. I could feel his opposite hand rubbing up my back until he reached the back of my neck and untied my dress. Fuck. He was playing right into my fantasy of fucking in an office on a desk -- and my boss no less.

He attempted to bring my other leg onto the desk as well, but I stopped him. I put my leg down and kneeled in front of him, then unbuckled his belt, unfastening and unzipping his pants; he stood, and I took them down. I could feel the heat from the bulge in his briefs against my face. I had half a mind to rub my cheek against its warmth; instead, I removed his dick through the hole, and bit my lip as my eyes lit up like a kid in the candy store whose parents told me I could have whatever I wanted.

"Mmmm... " I moaned as I licked up the length of his dick before I allowed the saliva overflowing from my mouth to fall on the head and made circles with them.

"So, what do you think?" He asked.

"Delicious," I answered.

"What?!" He asked puzzled.

"Huh?" I responded snapping back to the reality of him still sitting there on the desk and me standing in front of him not hearing a word he has spoken in the last couple of minutes.

"So, can you fill in for Princess Friday night or what? Something came up with her kid, and she can't make it." He asked again.

"Fill in Friday doing what exactly?" I had to ask. I was confused and almost ashamed since he probably told me the first time and I was off in la-la land deep throating his dick. On the other hand, I don't keep up with the other women's jobs; we all speak, keep each other safe, and mostly mind our business. "She's doing a private par. . ." I interjected. "No-can-do boss. You know after what happened to Ebony at Juniors bachelor party, I don't do private parties." I said in a sassy tone with my hands on my hips.

"Man, you're a complete fool." He suppressed a laugh. "It's one of our events, the usual crew but someone is paying us to host." He explained as he raised up from his makeshift seat. "Let me know what you decide by tomorrow. I'm going to ask a few of the other ladies as well as see who I may be able to spare from the other location." He finished as he walked out. I shortly followed once my memory jolted back to Mr. Brown who I spotted from a distance still sitting there sipping the drink about halfway done.

It must have really been a long time since I had sex for me to have daydreamed having sex with Rich. I had never even looked at him like that before, and now I find myself drooling over him like he was some sort of Adonis chiseled from clay and handcrafted by the Gods themselves.

Making my way back to Mr. Brown, suddenly I felt a hand touch my elbow. It gave me chills as it swiped down my arm and grabbed my wrist. I was rattled, almost too afraid to turn thinking it could be John. I immediately thought, 'What the fuck is doing here?' He had done so well in evading the police over the last couple of months that showing up here would be a huge mistake. I balled up my fist, ready to hit the shit out of his ass once I turned to engage, however, the minute I turned it was like my heart stopped and started racing at the same time. I was in complete and absolute shock and utter disbelief.

He raised his free hand using the index finger to gesture for me to come closer to him, I did. As I leaned in towards him the same hand that beckoned for me was used to outline my jawline, placed a soft touch to my

20

earlobe that held a small diamond stud to finally firmly grip the back of my neck as his lips damn near touched my other ear. "You look good, queen," Ezekiel whispered. Ezekiel, or Zeke as he was known, is, or was rather, my baby from high school. During those times, he wasn't sporting locs or an athletic, muscular physique. The years had been extremely kind and generous to him. Back in high school, he was a slightly skinny neighborhood kid that smoked his weight in weed and mostly kept to himself unless it was necessary to get his hands dirty -- by the time it was necessary, it wasn't pretty. I couldn't really talk much about people changing over the years when I was no exception; a lot about me had changed. I fell into chronic depression after the loss of the baby. Dealing with John made me put on weight, and then I lost a lot of weight, changed my hair, and my lifestyle. The only thing that stayed the same is my height, for the life of me I couldn't be taller than five feet three inches if someone paid me. "Thank you, you don't look too bad yourself." I whispered back making sure to cause my lips to accidentally on purpose graze his ear. "Oops," I said, faking embarrassment. I took the hand that he wasn't currently holding hostage and gently, yet playfully, wiped the small smear of red lipstick from his ear, allowing myself to play with his lobe.

Years later and I still had the hots for him. Then again, that could go back to the whole not-having-dick-in-a-LONG-time thing.

He chuckled. "What are you getting into tonight?" He asked, his soft brown eyes feeling like they were peering

21

through me. He looked me up and down, then licked his bottom lip. I wanted my clitoris to be pressed against his lips. Better yet, I wanted him sucking my juices from his bottom lip after he had just finished trying to suck all the juices from me. I glanced over to Mr. Brown who was about a quarter of the way done with the drink; drunkenly swaying to Cardi B's "She Bad" and appearing almost mesmerized by the live entertainment of the ladies sliding up and down the poles, touching and caressing each other and clapping their asses in full splits. "Oh, that's who you're here with?" Zeke asked brows raised in either shock or amazement, nodding his head as he noticed me checking on Mr. Brown. "Yes actually. Unfortunately, I am." I answered, rolling my eyes in my head. Zeke and I sat there a little while longer; exchanging innocent flirts he was laying on the charm heavy with his words. Had I had on panties, his eyes alone would've made me soak them. While I no doubt gave off my sexually charged energy, Zeke also got a splash of my intellectual side and wit while I seductively toyed with his hands, shoulders, and chest.

Mr. Brown finally consumed the remainder of his drink and appeared to be trying to get up. "Looks like your cue, guess you have to go take care of your grandfather," Zeke joked, laughing at himself. I wasn't finding it funny at all. "Don't be like that you know I was just kidding," he chuckled and grabbed my chin. I looked back over to Mr. Brown, I couldn't tell if he was looking for me or any female to leave with at this point; however, I gave Zeke a tight hug along with a kiss on the cheek and returned to Mr. Brown.

"There you go baby girl, Mr. Brown thought you forgot about him." He said as he grabbed my hand. "Of course not," I told him with a smirk, rolling my eyes in my head again.

ding You have an AirDrop from "ZEKE," do you accept?

Hell yeah, I fucking accept frantically pressing YES, getting ready to drop the phone from my hand.

Zeke: I'm mad you couldn't come with me, but that view while you were leaving though something serious *peach emoji *fire emoji*

I could tell he had me blushing and cheesing from ear to ear. I looked up to where he was sitting but didn't see him; he was still as corny as ever, but it was cute and endearing. I replied a blushing emoji. "Come on Mr. Brown, you ready to get out of here?" I asked, and as quickly as the words parted my lips, he almost jumped out of his skin in a rush to leave. He called his right-hand man Chauncey to pick us up. While we waited, I danced and on him as he did some sort of a two-step. Within ten minutes Chauncey had come in to get us. He never actually goes too far from Mr. Brown. Knowing him, he parked somewhere after picking up some food listening to the radio. They were the definition of loyal to each other, so I had to ensure Mr. Brown, and I did things that required exclusivity or things that Chauncey didn't care for to make sure he wasn't watching my every move. I knew I was in the wrong business since I was not the touchy-feely type, but Mr. Brown was overbearing with it to the point where he was suffocating and smothering.

We got into the black on black Lincoln Town car with, you guessed it, tinted windows. The thirty-minute ride with Mr. Brown fawning all over me, telling me how delicious I looked and describing how he prepared to tear my ass up was mildly entertaining. He was slurring his version of sexily inappropriate arousal banter with hot, alcohol-drenched breath, slobbering on my neck and collarbone and rolling my nipple between his fingers. Honestly, had I not been grossed out and felt like I had just been licked by an old dog, I may have been turned on. My nipples are my Achilles heel. Yet, I found myself licking the entire palm of my hand and giving his old ass a hand job. In a matter of minutes, he ejaculated. He finally started drifting off to sleep a block away from the Embassy Suites hotel he liked to frequent. Chauncey pulled up to the main hotel entrance, I asked for a napkin, and he asked me whether I would be accompanying Mr. Brown upstairs for the night. I gave him a very unmistakably contemptuous look and told him no. I got out and headed to the corner just to watch Chauncey whip the car around the half circle and down the garage.

I had already scheduled my Lyft to go home a few blocks before we arrived which timed perfectly because he had just pulled up. He got out confirmed my name and opened the door for me. Once inside, he offered water, mints, and whatever selection of music I wanted to ride to. I declined them all and informed him that the Jazz music he already had playing was perfect. I did ask him if he by any chance had hand sanitizer, and to my surprise, he did, thank God. The drive and the music caused me to drift into my own thoughts. I took out my cell re-reading the messages from Ezekiel and kept replaying seeing him at the club. I typed a message, then erased it. Typed a new one and erased it, too.

Me: It was great seeing you again.

I pressed send. "You're here," the driver says as he opens my door. He was making sure to earn those five stars. "Thank you," I told him with a smile as we parted. Immediately after entering the building I checked the mail.

ding

Zeke: Looking forward to seeing you again, hopefully, your grandfather won't be around to steal you away. LLS

Me: Me too and LOL no I'd make sure you only have that time *wink emoji*

At my apartment door, I was greeted with five long-stemmed white Calla Lilies in a glass vase next to it a folded-up piece of paper. Instinctively, I check my surroundings simultaneously unlocking my door;

stepping around the plant, I enter into my home replacing the locks and reactivating the security system before checking all the rooms with my metal bat in hand.

Me to group: 9-1-1 apartment

K to group: What's good sis? You aight?

Me to group: Calla Lilies. . .

K, Ronni, and Ci-Ci to group: OTW

Almost entranced, I could feel myself pacing back and forth on the stretch of hallway that separated the kitchen/dining room combination from my living room. I don't know if I was more frustrated or frightened. A little over an hour had passed, and I grew anxious waiting for everyone to arrive.

knock, knock, knock

"Sin it's us," K said in his deep raspy voice that always sounded like he needed to cough. K, short for Kevin, is this tall, husky, almost Albino looking man. He wasn't Albino, just super light complexioned -- probably because of his mixed lineage. He rocked locs down his back and believed strongly in three things: chicken, thick women, and weed; in no particular order. K and Ezekiel shared a similar philosophy to life: stay all the fuck out of the way,

26

and get to the money. K is my oldest friend, we knew each other since our sandbox days, and that's why we carry each other like brother and sister. We have seen each other through good and tough times.

Then there's Ronni, short for Veronica, a caramel-complexioned, petite framed firecracker who also sports locs. I met her early on in high school, and we've been kicking it together ever since. I looked through the peephole then let them in.

K came in holding a bong, unpacking weed and edibles. Ronni had two different kinds of wine and take out. Ci-Ci had liquor, some disposable red shot cups, and more take out. Each one of them had an overnight bag. By the time everyone came in, I noticed the plant was gone yet no one had it in their hands when they came in, guess one of them saw to trashing it beforehand.

"I told your ass you needed to move when this shit first started happening," Ronni stated angrily and aggressively as everyone started to make themselves comfortable on the two-toned chocolate microfiber sectional and love seat pieces that decorated my living space.

"I can't afford to move, y'all know how expensive D.C. is now." I told Ronni, taking back a shot of the brown liquor Ci-Ci started pouring.

"You act like you couldn't stay with one of us until you found somewhere else or until they had his miserable ass behind bars." Ronni retorted, coming back into the living room after rummaging through the cabinets for wine glasses.

"FACTS," K added, taking a long pull on his jay then offering it to Ronni who accepted and took pulls all while pouring the wine.

"And who knows exactly how long that would've been for either. Trust me, I know your offer is coming from a great place but I'm not going to inconvenience y'all or unintentionally put y'all in harm's way. I know y'all here tonight, but its all of us together and I honestly think it could just be some sick joke, I'll be fine when the police find out what's going on." I attempted to plead my case and stand my ground. Ronni rolled her eyes and sucked her teeth. I took another shot then started pinching from the snickerdoodle edible.

Ci-Ci contributed taking her turn with the jay. "You're not fine though. You're trying to sweep it under the rug as some sick joke, but you ain't sure who playing it. I for one think we all can agree on who we think it is and who knows what this sick bastard is capable of; first, he robbed you and now he is tormenting you with your favorite flower and a note saying that he misses you and some other big wild shit not to mention all the bullshit before all that." I just kind of sat there not really knowing what to say, taking yet another shot.

K sparked another jay. "The fact is sis," K took a pull. "We want you to be straight and the legal system fucked

28

up." He took another hit. "How long its been and they ain't made NO headway on finding his ass? We know you're smart and can look out for you, but we trying to help you." He offered me the jay, which I quickly declined. I chuckled a little in my head thinking about me turning down smoking when I made that a part of my curriculum in high school. Now, I was more of a social drinker. Everything they said spoke volumes though, and I appreciated all their concern. Aside from discussing me needing to move, staying with one of them or investing in a gun, we all pretty much hung out, caught each other up on the latest in our lives and that opened the floor for me to sneak in running into Ezekiel and the jokes he cracked about Mr. Brown.

"Aww shit playa, playa, your boo back," K joked passing the jay to Ci-Ci then opened one of the take-out containers and began to devour the chicken and fries. We continued enjoying each other's company until one by one we passed out. The next morning, we all had a big breakfast, courtesy of yours truly, that included pancakes, grits, bacon, sausage, home fries, and scrambled eggs accompanied with water and orange juice with no pulp (because who the fuck really wants shit floating around in their mouth). I watched as they all scrambled around getting ready and helping clean up our mess from last night, I felt blessed to have them. It meant a lot knowing that people cared for me and were willing to drop everything to help me. I'm convinced they felt the same way about me.

By the time everyone cleared out, I had placed a call to the detective assigned to my case, Detective Thomas -- who is a tall dark complexioned, soft-spoken and slenderly built man -- and enlightened him on the recent taunt. He assured me he was doing everything within his power to locate John and see to it I found justice. Justice maybe... but would I ever get back my peace of mind? Would I feel any safer? He asked me had I been to the courts and filed a restraint or stay away order, which I did, then just asked that I allowed him and the legal system some time. Of course, I rolled my eyes, I knew what that meant. If it was really John or whoever the culprit was, the only way I would see any justice was if something heinous happened to one of us. I prayed to the universe that something happened to him instead of me. I reluctantly thanked Detective Thomas, and we got off the phone.

I needed to study and go about my day.

Chapter Three

Almost a week had passed since the Calla Lilies; my friends were keeping me grounded, the two classes I could afford to pay out of pocket were keeping me busy, the club was keeping me distracted, and Zeke was keeping me smiling. I wasn't back at one hundred percent, but I wasn't about to allow some taunts to keep me from remaining focused. Whoever had been sending them had been doing so for months, and who knows, it may not even be John. Mr. Brown knows my address from the couple of times he had Chauncey scoop me up and could've had them pre-delivered. I did fail to mention that small detail when the crew was over. It didn't seem like they needed to know -- plus I didn't want it to be made a spectacle and have to hear about that, too. Either way, I needed to get over being in fear. Yet it did still bother me through the occasional nightmares or the creeping suspensions of being watched and followed.

ding

I jumped. The vibration and sound of the phone startled me.

Zeke: Free up your time tonight. I'm taking you out, be ready by seven.

Me: Where are we going, so I'll know what to wear.

Zeke: Don't matter. I'm hoping it'll end up on the floor.

Me: *blushing emoji* *heart emoji*

Did he just tell me to be ready? Didn't ask, just straight up told me. Admittedly, I was taken by him over the last couple of days with the calls and text. He even came out to the event I was working the other night, luckily, I ended up bartending while the usual bartender was hosting and MCing. I didn't have the heart to explain everything to him just yet, and quite frankly, didn't feel the need to until I saw how everything would play itself out.

"What are you over there all smiles about?" Ci-Ci asked, peeking over. We were sitting side by side in the massage pedicure chairs getting our dogs done as we did monthly. "Zeke... he texted me to tell me to be ready by seven, he's taking me out." I informed her, more than likely blushing and cheesing, strangely feeling like I had butterflies in my stomach. I started shifting between the chair's settings, I set it to knead my entire back and vibrate under my ass.

"Niggas do that? Fuck he from and where his brothers at?" She asked, jokingly flustered. I handed the tech the red polish I selected, trying to take small steps away from always selecting variations of pink. I slowly sank into the chair, allowing my booty to be caressed by the machinery through my yoga pants. "I'm as shocked as you. Usually, it's 'when can we chill, link up, come over, see you,' or something else which in reality means can I fuck; you know he has brothers though, he says they're good and getting themselves together," I tell her, laughing at myself.

Almost preaching, Ci-Ci said, "You ain't lying. These niggas rather sell a million dreams and play games rather than tell a bitch the truth -- which could ultimately get them laid just the same, if not quicker." I was right there with her throwing up my praise hand to her testament. She continued, "Don't get me wrong, he was cool in high school... it's just a lot of these fuck boys and niggas messing it up for the kings. It's getting really hard to tell who is who." I knew her concern and sermon weren't intended to be malicious. That was the great thing about her, Ronni, and K -- we all are different with strong personalities, and we all bring something unique to our group, but we understood each other and could keep it real without taking offense or passing judgment. Mind you, there are some things I withhold from them, and I'm sure they do the same, but for the most part, we knew every detail of each other's lives. Them more so than I because I was a little more blatant and graphic with the details of my endeavors, plus with my lifestyle, they kind of need to know just in case things pop off.

"The fault is not just theirs though," I started. "We as women also have to be held accountable for the role we play in the mistreatment of our queens... we have to be mindful of the vibes and energies we give off, as well as not accepting any old bullshit they try to give to us." I finished just as our toes were done being polished and dried under the LED dryer. We simultaneously walked over to the manicure stations as the techs followed with our shoes. "So, what... it's our fault that these men aren't men? I mean, I get what you're saying, but these some grown ass men. They should know how to treat women. They know how they want their ugly ass sisters and fat ass mommas treated." She said letting out a devilish ass cackle. I couldn't help but giggle a little to myself, I can't even deny the shit being funny.

"You dead ass wrong for that, but you know exactly what I'm saying. One, they either lacked or had no proper maternal guidance, then if they did have a mother they might not have had a father -- at least not one that they could admire that could teach them what it's like to love and respect a woman. Two, the standard for women; approaching, courting, dating and marrying a woman has been shattered because we live in the ease of the technological "hook-up" age. We have ass, titties, and dick on demand with a simple click or like of a picture, then a DM. Boom, you have sex delivered like a lunch platter from UberEATS or Post Mates." I said giving her

34

the side eye. She knows it's just that easy for men and women to hook-up nowadays, so what use is it for a man to spend his time or energy getting to know one female when the next would be hot n' ready like Little Caesars. "Honestly, think about it if more women started to require more from men; calls versus texts, dates over chilling and hooking-up, and whatever else, men would have to work harder and come stronger. Then the women raising sons must raise them with a future husband and king in mind, that's not all on the fathers." I continued. "It's one thing to say 'I want a man that checks all of my boxes', but what boxes are we checking for them? Which brings me to another point -- a man only going to do right for a woman he sees a future with, period. So, that man stepping up shit and us not being hook-ups shit not really going to matter if he didn't have any intentions on being with us from the jump." The techs were polishing our nails. "That's true." She agreed, examining her nails making sure they were on point. "I know I'm just done playing the games." She started sliding her hands in the LED dryer.

"Games? I thought things were going well between you and Mr. D... you sounded genuinely happy when you spoke of him." I was confused that we were even discussing no good men when last I checked, she was swooning over D.

"We're good, just in a case of phone tag and see you when I see you. Our schedules have been hectic." She explained.

"Oh, so your horny ass is backed up and taking it out on all men," I laughed. Her ass needed to be laid worse than me. She rolled her eyes and sucked her teeth at me.

"Fuck men!" She uttered disgruntledly. I laughed and shook my head, watching her step off to pay the bill.

ring

"Hello?" I answered. No one responded, so I hung up.

"Who was that?" Ci-Ci asked as she walked back to the table where I remained sitting to ensure my nails were completely dry. I had a bad case of messing my nails up as soon as I got them done. "I'm not sure," I told her. She looked confused. "Someone called from a blocked number, didn't say anything, and I hung up." A look of worry consumed Ci-Ci's face.

"And that shit didn't bother you given the mysterious flowers?" She asked sternly. I ignored her comment. We both got into her truck, and she pulled off. Her speakers were blaring trap music; for some reason that was her go to music while driving, and now that I think about it, might've been the cause for her road rage. Once she was home in her own apartment, she was a completely different person, more into her element. She listened to mellow love songs. I guess it's true what they say about not judging a book by its cover. I did start to think maybe the flowers and calls could be correlated. What were the odds of it being a wrong number, scam, bill collector or someone trying to reach me but ended up losing service?

We finally arrived at my apartment and exchanged our goodbye's. I grabbed all my bags from us going shopping before getting our nails done and went into my home. Inside the apartment, in my bedroom, I started fumbling around in my six-drawer mahogany dresser trying to find the perfect matching bra and panty set to go on this surprise date with Zeke. He hadn't been around in a while, so he wasn't aware that the concept of time was lost on me. I don't care how well or far in advance something is planned, some way, somehow, I will manage to be late. So, me asking where we were going was as much for me as it was for him, at least knowing where we were going I'd know what to put on and it would possibly cut down half the time of choosing an outfit and styling my hair. I digress. Who am I kidding? It's me; I'd be late anyway. My mother used to say, 'You would be late to your own funeral.'

Soon I found myself scavenging through my closet for an outfit and shoes. I picked up the phone and placed a quick call to Ronni. She is an armed security officer and spent time here and there at the gun range, so I decided to take her up on her offer to take me. We arranged to go early Saturday morning, she figured it would be easier to teach me if no one else was there. A few hours had passed, and I had managed to procrastinate the hell out of my time. Three hours I spent sucked into YouTube videos by the late great Dick Gregory, Taj Tarik Bey, Dr. Jose Pimienta-Bey and other influential people. About an

37

hour before seven and I had to get showered, moisturized, clothed, and out the door. I managed to get everything done except for my hair, which I was currently attempting to frantically arrange in a neat, but messy bun. I brushed my teeth with the activated black charcoal toothpaste. Looking up into the bathroom mirror, I smiled at myself, toothpaste foaming from my mouth, holding the toothbrush in it and all, I smiled. I was truly ecstatic. I couldn't recall the last time I was smitten about someone or feeling like a schoolgirl getting ready to face her crush.

ding

Zeke shared his location.

Shit, shit, shit. I chartered a Lyft to the destination he sent. Within minutes the Lyft had arrived, luckily I had finished on time and was on my way. Being under pressure brings out the best in me and, not to toot my own horn, but I looked, smelled, and felt damn good. Arriving at the location, I took note of it being a quaint little hole in the wall.

"You shouldn't be out here by yourself," a familiar voice spoke out to me.

"Well, I wouldn't be if my date knew I had just arrived," I responded, smiling at Ezekiel walking up holding a singular red long-stemmed rose dressed in a cream-colored button-up, black slacks, and a clean pair of black Kenneth Cole Oxfords. His locs were still pinned up from the last time I saw him, but his shape up was fresh. He was wearing some cologne or oil I couldn't pinpoint, although it was extremely intoxicating.

"I feel underdressed. Thank you," I expressed as he partially broke the rose and fixed it in my hair. I blushed. I couldn't help but feel like a little girl.

"You're tripping queen, you look perfect." He flashed me a smile along with a wink, then directed me inside the establishment, holding the door as I went in. Truthfully, I felt appropriately dressed in my acid washed black jeans, six-inch red heels, and red off the shoulder half-sleeved crop top after entering the building. It was a jazz club; people were rapping, reciting spoken word, singing, and just freely expressing themselves while we and other patrons drank, snapped, and blew hookah. The place even allowed the weed smokers to smoke. "You look like you love it here," Zeke whispered to me, probably noticing the look of awe and amazement written on my face.

"I do," I told him. "There's something liberating about watching these people speak their truths through art... no fear of judgment or consequences, just their voices." I added.

"I figured you'd enjoy yourself. Come on." He grabbed my hand and led me out the door then into his car. On the sound system he played the slow I-want-to-make-love-and-I'm-trying-to-put -a-baby-in-you type of R&B. He had placed his hand on my thigh until I interlocked my fingers with his, frequently catching him glancing over at me. Me? Hell, I was full-fledged staring at him, studying the man -- the king -- he had become, trying to read his energy and aura. I was asking myself whether this was even happening. I thought, 'Is this even real? Do you even have a fucking clue where he's taking you?'

"You okay? You seem nervous," Zeke asked still driving. Uh, yeah nigga I am starting to feel like he had been driving for an eternity. "Anxious, I suppose... it seems like we've been driving for a while. It looks pitch black out and I can't really place where we are." I adjusted myself in the seat still holding his free hand in mine, at least if I was holding his hand he wasn't reaching for a gun or knife. Fuck, bitch what did you get yourself into?

"You're good ma," He told me then raised our hands and kissed the back of mine. He flashed those white teeth through his handsome smile. Unfortunately, as attractive as it was, I wasn't feeling it. Trying to put my mind at ease, I started to convince myself. This is Zeke, you know him, you know he's not capable of hurting you, and once upon a time, y'all loved each other. Just in case in something wild happened, I took my phone out and shared my location with the group. It has been years, and people really do change. "Loosen up," he suggested. "Your grip tight as hell on my hand."

I chuckled, thinking he was telling me to relax. Immediately after I loosened the hold I had on his hand, he hopped out the car and went to the trunk before getting to my door. Peering out of the window, I could make out a boardwalk and water. He opened my door with what looked like a blanket tossed over his arm. "You might want to take these off," he said as he started unfastening and removing my heels. What in the horror movie was going on here? Was the blanket to wrap my dead, lifeless body in? Did he remove my heels as a scare tactic or to have me trip over my own feet like every White woman in every horror movie ever made? Seriously, what did Stephen King, Jr. have planned?

I finally worked up the courage to ask with a hint of nervousness. "What's going on?"

"Come on, you'll see." He extended his hand to me. When looking down to ensure I didn't step on anything, I noticed he was shoeless, too. He took my hand then guided me across the blades of grass that felt wet and then, of course, the sand. It was cold and gritty, yet wildly, had a nice feeling between my toes. In the distance, I could see people spread throughout the beach, the moon's reflection on the water, and the lights illuminating from the hotel and a few other businesses. "Still scared?" He asked, breaking the silence.

"Not entirely, how did you know I was?" I asked, giggling a little.

"Well one, you basically tried to break my hand and two, I peeped you sharing your location in the reflection of the car window when we were at the light." He laughed, flashing that damn smile. His cute dimple showed up when he laughed.

"Guilty! Look I have been having a lot of weird things going on and pretty much everything you were doing had murder written all over it," we both laughed. I let out a deep sigh of relief, happy to find solace in the fact that his grand romantic gesture was simply that -- romantic. He asked me about what was going on that had me so uptight and on edge. I explained to him that it wasn't a first date conversation and how much I would rather just spend the time relishing the moment. He rebutted saying something about the first date, tenth, or one hundredth, at some point we'd need to talk about it. The next thing I knew, I was giving him the briefest version I could fathom about John, the break-in and robbery, the mysterious flowers, and, as of lately, the calls. "Ready to run for the hills?" I asked with a nervous chuckle, attempting to fight back tears. I knew it was a lot for me to unload on him and I assumed it would be too much for him to process, let alone want to deal with especially so soon. I hadn't even realized that at some point we had stopped, he's standing directly in front of me looking me in my tear-filled eyes then used his thumb to wipe the one that rolled down my face away as he spoke.

"We all got baggage ma. Yeah, yours a little heavy right now, but these muscles ain't for play." He flexed his muscles and at that moment, I could've literally died laughing at him. As corny as he was, he lightened the mood. He put down the blanket and our shoes, and we started down the beach. Our toes embraced the wet sand, feeling mushy beneath our feet. We proceeded further down, letting our feet, ankles, calves, and clothes become submerged in the cold waters as the waves gently splashed against us.

splash

Oh HELL NO. "Not the hair, not the hair!" I yelled at him. Being splashed with water I could feel drenching my backside, I turned around and instantly returned the favor.

"Aight, aight you got it." He conceded, not expecting me to retaliate so ferociously.

splash

No. He. Didn't.

He splashed me again, this time wetting my entire front side. I wasn't surprised, yet still very much surprised. Before I was even able to splash him again, he grabbed hold of me in an extremely tight bear hug locking my arms to my sides, looked down at me then kissed my forehead. He lifted me up just as he had me, carried me to the blanket, and instructed me to sit down with my legs crossed and eyes closed. He told me to clear my mind. All I was supposed to do was bask in the rays of the full moon, listen to the sounds of the environment, and his voice and breath, so I entertained him. He explained that the whole process of walking barefoot in the grass, sand, and water was to reconnect ourselves with nature. He continued further elaborating that women absorb their powers from the moon. I wasn't exactly sure what form of hippie bullshit he was spitting, but looking at him being and sounding so passionate about teaching it to me was such a fucking turn on. Other than wanting to know what strand of weed he smoked, overall the night was exceptionally wonderful. We made our way to the hotel. En route, he disposed of the sand covered blanket. I spotted a twenty-four-hour deli adjacent to the hotel and asked him if I could get him anything. He began breaking down his dietary restrictions and how he didn't eat anything that was killed for human consumption. Oh, he one of those types of people now, so the safest bet would be to get his ass bottled water. He said he would go ahead to check us in while I shopped. In the store, I did manage to find some seaweed and veggie chips since I wasn't sure which he would've preferred. Neither of us at anything and I grew quite peckish. The worst thing possible is food shopping on an empty stomach; I was so indecisive I picked up and put stuff down reading calories and ingredients until I settled on a couple of pieces of fruit, bottled tea, and water.

ding

Zeke: Room 318 door open.

That had to be his way of telling me to hurry my ass up and make my way to him. I scurried on the balls of my feet through the lobby up to the elevator and into the room, where I was greeted by him standing in the middle of a candlelit room. A white towel was wrapped around his waist as he stood looking out of the sliding glass doors. The vertical blinds were completely drawn and led to a balcony.

He stood there looking Vin Diesel or The Rock -- cut up with a fully-colored, open-mouthed lion wearing a crown tattooed across his entire back. Fuck. I entered completely, locking the door and putting the stuff down on the closest table. "I wasn't sure what to get you," I informed him as he walked up and looked through the bag. I could see his lips moving, but fell death to whatever the fuck he was saying. My eyes examined his body, taking mental photos of every muscle, mark, and tattoo. I tried my hardest to restrain from looking at his dick print. Then it jumped. Fuck I looked. I quickly darted my eyes away. Then I saw his dick twitch again. I wasn't sure whether it was reflexes or if he did it intentionally, but it had my full undivided attention. Of course, I had to fucking look and quickly regretted doing so. I WAS NOT READY.

"I ran you some water," he informed me, pointing off to the side of the room where a jetted tub was bubbling next to a glass shower and other amenities; the thing the captured my eyes the most were the massive mirrors over the dual sinks. He sat up in the king-sized bed multitasking between rolling weed and eating what I could only imagine were some nasty ass chips. As I started undressing, I heard music begin to play. I looked over at him and playfully rolled my eyes as we both laughed. Since I had already removed my top, I strip teased out of my jeans; caressing my legs, smacking my ass, and flexing my cheeks so he'd witness the jiggle. I flung my seamless Victoria Secret cheekies at him once I had them off. He sparked his jay and watched my every motion, from the seductive moves I attempted by lifting my leg and rubbing the suds of the bubbles from my thighs to my toes, to caressing myself in the tub. Getting out of the tub dripping wet, I model walked into the shower and pressed my soap covered ass against the glass of the shower while I was washed and licked my own nipple after rinsing off. I didn't even bother with drying, I let my hair down and sauntered my way directly to him; on my way to him, he swung open his towel. My God.

My little heart was thumping, adrenaline was pumping, and my nerves were everywhere. The only thing I wanted to focus on was engulfing his entire manhood with my mouth and digesting his nut-- even if I had to die trying. Using my hands, I massaged from his feet to his knees. I used my tongue to lick from one of his knees to his balls, where I gently took one, then the other, in my mouth. The second jay he was currently smoking, he immediately extinguished in the bedside ashtray. Zeke wiped my hair from my face to view the festivities. I was still slowly sucking and licking on each of his balls then gently started massaging his dick while I used my other hand to caress his abdomen. "Come sit on it," he requested

46

taking a hold of his dick, and I ignored him, raising up to kiss it then he playfully smacked it across my lips.

"Come on," he pleaded, rubbing it around my lips and cheeks; I ignored him opening my mouth like a king cobra ready to devour its prey, saliva dangling from my mouth to the head of his dick. Slowly, I took in several inches until I gagged still trying to go an inch further. I was making it my mission to deep throat him tonight. I tried it once again, heard him moan then decided to suck on the head and do circles with my tongue while it was in my mouth for a few seconds.

"Mmmm," I moaned gently, massaging his balls while playing with myself. Kissing up one side, licking down the other, alternating kissing down then licking up before taking him in my mouth again. This time I inched down a little further. "Damn girl," he said as he smacked my ass. The more I played with myself, the closer I got to cumming and inattentively caused me to suck his dick more passionately and intense. Once I came, I used the hand soaked with my juices to stroke his dick as I licked and sucked the head.

"Fuck, girl," he expressed his dick jumping in my mouth, I was awaiting the gush of nut to overflow in my mouth. Nothing. The fuck? So, he one of those men, the rare unicorns that don't cum from head, yet still took pleasure in the act of receiving head. Good, I love giving head, and I also love a challenge. A lot has changed, and I was enjoying every inch of it.

I paused from giving him head to reach for the condoms he placed on the side table. My jaws began to hurt anyways. No cumming from head, that delicious dicked bastard. "Shit," I moaned, standing in a squat position trying to ease his dick into my dripping tight vagina. I thought the length was going to kill me, but it's the width that was out to destroy me. After a few seconds and finally working his dick in, I showed him just what type of hoe my mother birthed.

I loved being able to unleash my inner naughty side; bouncing and dropping on him, grinding my little pussy when he was fully inside my glorious walls, constricting them and playing with my clitoris as he sucked and licked on my nipples. I was moaning shit, and he was moaning fuck, his dick was throbbing inside me.

"Fuck baby, I'm about to cum," he managed through a moan -- as if he didn't have a condom on -- and ejaculated.

Chapter Four

I don't even recall falling asleep last night, however, the warmth of the sun beaming in from the balcony doors in combination with the small sweet kisses creeping up the back of my legs, thighs, and ass was such a marvelous thing to wake up to.

"Grand rising queen," Zeke greeted me in between kisses. "Are you up?" I shook my head yes as I stretched. Next thing I know, he spread my legs and licked me from clitoris to asshole and back again. This no cumming from head, delicious dicked bastard is nasty, too. Praise God. He tapped on my ass, and I raised up getting into doggy style expecting him to kill my little pussy from the back, but he continued eating me out -- licking and sucking on my clitoris while it felt like his nose was poking my asshole. If I wasn't religious before, he was taking me to church this blessed morning. My body was quivering and shaking from cumming, I was feeling my knees buckling and about to break down. "Ahh shit," I moaned, cumming again.

"Damn you taste good," he said. "Hand me a condom," he told me squeezing and rubbing my ass while rubbing my clitoris and penetrating my vagina with his thumb. He took a beat to put on the condom, then was right back in motion sliding his dick in as I pushed back, matching his rhythm.

smack

His hand contacted my ass, and I kept fucking back. "Shit," he exclaimed grabbing a hold of my waist and shoulder then I felt his dick throbbing against my walls. "Fuck!" he said as he rolled over onto the bed, on his back then lit his jay. I crawled up to him; kissing up his abdomen, chest, neck, and chin until I reached his mouth then inhaled the smoke after he took a pull. He wanted to lay up and order room service until check-out, but I told him about the plans I made with Ronni.

We collected our things and left the same way we came -- walking barefoot through the sand, water, and grass. During the drive to my apartment, we discussed how much fun we had with each other and how we looked forward to seeing each other again. We filled each other in on what we had been up to over the years; he told me about his construction job and wanting to start his own construction business -- which he already started breaking ground on with his brothers, Jeremiah and Isaiah -- and I told him about me being in college and wanting to own my own boutique. We parked in front of the building, told each other see you later and kissed goodbye. That turned into a full-blown make-out session;

both of us explored the other's mouth with our tongue... never mind the fact I was sucking his dick, and he was eating my ass and pussy some hours prior and neither of us bothered to see if they had the complimentary toothpaste and mouthwash in the bathroom. I start rubbing his dick through his pants and tried to find my way in them while he is caressing my titties and pinching my nipples.

"You're starting shit," he said while looking at me licking his lips.

"Come up for a quickie," I suggested, wiping sand off my feet to slide on my shoes. We both walked into the apartment. Before I knew it, he was sliding down my pants and panties, dropping his, bending me over the back of the couch, gently, yet firmly choking me, and going to town on my little pussy with deep, long, aggressive strokes while working his thumb into my butthole.

"Oh my God yes," I moaned as a gush of squirt ran down my legs and the back of the couch. Once he managed to work his whole thumb in my butt, he removed it then started working his dick in. "Awe fuck," I moaned from the pain and the pleasure. Shit. Shit. Shit. "Awe fuck," I moaned again.

"You like this dick?" he asked. Nigga I love it and you. "Yesss," I moaned attempting to fuck back since I didn't have any real leverage from how he had me flung over the top.

"Shit, baby I'm about to cum," he stated, his dick throbbing in my ass as his warm juices filled me up. He let me down.

ding

Ronni: Are you ready? OTW.

Me: I'm going to get dropped off.

Ronni: Don't be late. *eye roll emoji*

I asked Zeke if he could see me to the gun range and he agreed. Before we left, I offered him some linens so he could get himself cleaned up after I got out of the shower, brushed my teeth, washed my face, and got dressed. While he was getting himself together, I cleaned up the mess we made and prepped some fruit and water to go. Shortly after, we were out the door and gone. The ride this time was much quieter since I dozed off to sleep while he rubbed on my leg. When it came to car rides, I was a child.

ding

Ronni: You here yet?

Me: Just pulled up. *big smile emoji*

Ronni was standing out front wearing a Tupac designer tee, blue jeans, and tennis shoes. Zeke and I kissed, then I got out wearing dark grey sweatpants, a black tank top, and a pair of tennis shoes. Zeke honked the horn. We both waved as he pulled off and we entered the facility. "Now I see why your hot-in-the-ass-self was late," she snapped laughing as she checked us in and picked out guns. "Was that Zeke?" She asked, a little shocked.

"Yes girl," I answered drowsily.

"Your ass looks and sound like hell, your boo just dropped you off... what the hell y'all nasty asses get into last night?" She asked laughing, but it was a late night early morning type of thing.

"Girl you know I had been in such a fucking drought, and he unleashed the freak, I need him like twice a day," I responded laughing and cheesing as we walked into the back putting on the noise-canceling earmuffs. The first round she wanted to gauge where I was at, then she showed me how to handle the gun, use the safety, and gave me pointers for aiming for the heart and head. She also explained that it's going to be extremely different being in the moment if it comes a time for me to use one versus hitting a steady paper target. We had finished up, and I asked her to stop for something to eat before taking me home. During the ride, I told her all about the date and why I shared my location. Her ass died laughing at me then expressed how glad she was that I wasn't in danger. "He sounds like he tamed enough of that ass," she said laughing.

"I don't know, I hope so," I responded, we sat in the car eating the food, talking about our boos and classes.

"Make sure you find time to do that work, don't get this far and start fucking up," she stressed, and we agreed on a study date for Wednesday nights after our classes. Ronni started back driving and she suggested we meet up to go a few more times for practice, or at least until I got up the ability to do a headshot. I agreed. "You supposed to work tonight?" she asked. I lifted my head up from the window. "From how you look, you going to need a lot of fucking rest." She wasn't lying, I was worn out. Totally beat, he did a number on me. I got out of her car, waved goodbye, checked the mail, went into my apartment, and plopped down onto the couch. Me and mornings do not mix. Ever. I had finally gotten comfortable and was ready to knock the fuck out.

ring

FUCK! "Hello?" I said. No answer, I hung up.

ring

I swear to fucking God. "HELLO!" I screamed into the phone.

"Eww, the fuck wrong with you?" Ci-Ci asked agitatedly.

"Aww shit my bad, somebody called right before you and didn't say anything," I told her, feeling bad that I just screamed at her.

"You need to get your fucking number changed or something." The phone went quiet for a second as I drifted off. "Well, I called so you could fill me in about this date," she spoke with excitement intrigued to find out what took place. I attempted to give her the shortest most detailed version as possible then telling her I would tell her the rest later when I woke up.

A few hours had passed, and I woke up feeling completely refreshed. I returned the call to Ci-Ci and started filling her in with all the juicy details before another call clicked in. It was Zeke.

"How are you? Did you get some rest?" I got up starting to get myself ready for the club.

"Yes, I did, eventually," I answered. "Did you?" I asked, checking on him. He explained that he got an hour or two in after he got home and showered, but ended up having to run errands and take care of business with his brothers. Vexed about what errands he had to run and business that he needed taken care of on a Saturday, I inquired about it. The only thing he said about it was 'a little this, a little that.' Since I sensed him being deflective I decided to drop it. It must've been something he couldn't discuss over the phone or maybe it was just best I didn't know and mind my business.

"You're not about to have me out here addicted to you." He flirted. I giggled. He talking about he not about to be addicted to me, my pussy and ass hadn't stopped throbbing for hours after we left each other. In fact, they seemed to throb and get moist every time his name was mentioned, or whenever I thought about him. I was pretty sure I was the one developing an addiction.

"Addicted? You running game on me?" I chuckled. "You don't have to run game on me beloved, just keep it one hundred, and we should be good," I finished. He reassured me that he wasn't running game, that he fucked with me and offered me a ride to work. I declined, but I still needed to get ready because my ass was running behind as usual

Chapter Five

A little over a month has passed and things have been complete bliss besides the constant calls and monthly Calla Lilies. I spoke with Detective Thomas again, he asked that I kept him informed with everything that occurred and he'd do the same if there were any new developments in my case. I was so fed up with this bullshit, exactly how hard could it be to find one man? Then again with all the missing persons cases, I'm not feeling too bad about not getting priority. And with no proof or tangible evidence other than those flowers that once brought me joy, there isn't much to go on. Classes were coming along fine; Ronni and I were heading towards mid-terms and thanks to her, I was becoming a better shot. She did insist that I practiced on moving targets, though. I'm not ready for all that yet. The nights at the club were picking up, so the money started getting better, but I still didn't have enough to cover opening the shop -- just enough to allow me to buy some materials to create a few pieces here and there and sell them on my social media accounts as well as around the neighborhood. K and I had decided to meet up and workout. We agreed to try to keep up with a routine. We jogged... well, that's a complete lie. Our lazy, out-of-shape asses walked the trail of a park.

"Ready to call it quits," I asked him after noticing our pace slowed down and our faces were drenched in sweat.

"Fuck yeah man I'm tired as shit," he said panting. We were out there for two hours and he told me about a chick he had recently been hitting it off with, the work he was doing at his new job, and how he had to resign from the old one after having to put his hands on two of the guys that thought shit was sweet when they kept trying him. "Yeah, I had to knock their bitch asses out. They kept running their mouths," he expressed with a hint of tension. "They weren't doing their part and tried to put the shit on me. Then when I confronted them about it, they go to the boss lying on me about shit." He continued, we sat on the bench trying to catch our breaths. "So, what's been up with you playa, haven't heard or seen much of you since you linked up with your boo," he asked nudging me.

"Everything good, I fuck with him," I said lowering my head to hide my blushing. "We're supposed to be doing lunch once I finish up with you."

"Aw shit playa, don't let me find out you're falling in love," he joked laughing. "We're going to have to revoke your player card, you keep it up out here," he proceeded with his wisecracks.

"Shut up," I told him as we started out of the park. "I'm not reading too much into it but yeah I like him," I confessed coyly. Just then, two beautiful women came jogging by their voluptuously perky titties bouncing up and down, nipples hard peeking through their tank tops and sports bra.

"Morning beautiful," I spoke.

"Morning queens," K spoke as both women smiled.

"Excuse me, you jog out here often?" I asked one of them. "Sometimes I be in need of a partner when my brother leaves me hanging, do you mind?" I asked flirtatiously as she giggled and gave me her name and number. I rejoined K so we could carry on.

"Man, your wild ass just like a nigga," he mentioned. This was something he mentioned every time he felt like I did something a man would do.

"I like what I like and worst they can say is no," I shrugged.

"FACTS," K said. We shared a Lyft to our apartments. At the apartment I got ready and called Zeke to pick me up. Zeke took me to a nice local Bistro where he opted for us to enjoy lunch on the patio. We seated ourselves and mulled over the menu. While we were still trying to figure out what we wanted to eat, it was me that hadn't selected anything, he kept it safe with a salad and water with lemon. He was exhibiting an extreme amount of patience utilizing the time to teach me about aligning chakras, chakra stones, smudging and meditating. Finally, I elected to have a panini and sweet tea, he left to place the order.

"I thought that was you," an eerie feeling crept over me. A chill fell down my spine and my heart sank into my stomach. "You've become a hard person to catch up with," John said. I quickly stood to face him.

"What the hell do you want?" I asked aggressively, trying to keep my composure seeing as how we are in public and he'd be stupid to do something where witnesses are present.

"Fuck you think I want... YOU!" He based at me, grabbing ahold of my arm.

"Yeah that's dead, and you have some fucking nerve after you robbed me and leaving those flowers and the constant blocked calls," I snapped yanking my arm from him. "How the fuck did you even find me? How did you know I was here?" I asked stunned. Had his ass been following me, watching me this whole time?

"I happened to be in the area, consider it a happy little coincidence." He said half wickedly with a sinister grin.

"Get the fuck John, for real." I spewed at him full of aggression and rage, my fist balled at my side attempting to fight the urge to knock the shit out of him.

"You okay queen?" Ezekiel asked as he placed the drinks down.

"Everything good cuz, she's good," John spoke on my behalf mugging on Zeke.

"I wasn't asking you 'cuz' I was speaking to my lady," Zeke shot back attempting to step around me. I grabbed his wrist. "Oh, this you now Sindel?" John scoffed. "I see how you moving now." He stood there laughing, I placed my hand on Zeke's chest insisting that we leave due to the people who were staring and an employee that looked to be making his way to us. "Listen to her cuz, be smart. I'll be seeing y'all around," John yelled at us as we were leaving.

"I'll make sure of that," Zeke said while I tried my hardest to push him towards his car. The drive was unusually quiet for us; he pretty much stayed to himself with laser focus on the road, brooding out of the window. We arrived at his place, we both agreed I should crash with him for a little while those were about the only words we exchanged with each other.

"How long do you plan to be mad at me?" I asked fresh out of the shower, towel wrapped around my chest. "I can't stand this silence between us," I revealed, walking up to him in the living room where he was sitting in a black leather reclining chair. The room was dimly lit by five or six candles, smelled of sage, and was devoid of sound except for the vibration frequencies softly playing over the surround system. "I'm not mad at you," he spoke calmly opening his eyes. "I am pissed with the situation, just thinking, trying to clear my mind," he took a deep long sigh.

"You mind if I distract you?" I leaned over to place a kiss on his forehead, then stood back up and dropped the towel. He grabbed my hand, pulling me to him and I straddled him. I planted soft small sweet kisses on his forehead, nose, and lips then licked up the side of his face. I kissed him again, my tongue now invading his mouth. His hands wandered all over my body like he was reading Braille. Every encounter with him felt like it was our first time. He began fingering me and took his dick out of his pants, then slowly pushed me down onto it. I lowered myself onto him, then raised myself up and lowered myself, again, and again, and again.

"Stop teasing me," he said, then kissed me as he smacked my ass. I bit his bottom lip. I got up to make the chair recline and got back on top of him straddled in a reverse cowgirl.

"Awe fuck baby," he moaned, smacking my ass as it bounced and jiggled. I bounced my pussy up and down, tightening my vaginal muscles. "Fuck you feel so good," I moaned, cumming on his dick. He inserted his thumb in my ass, and before I knew it, I was fucking both. Although I've never been a fan of two men, one-woman threesomes, I've always had a fondness for dual penetration and multiple stimulations. "Fuck me baby, fuck me," I moaned, and he went off, pounding my pretty little pussy like he just got released from doing a ten-year bid upstate. In between the strokes, I began to release a stream of squirt. "Awe yesss," I moaned.

He let go of my ass, took hold of my arms to pull me back up from being bent over and grabbed on to my waist then went ham again. "Yesss baby yesss," I moaned, unable to control myself, biting my lip and rolling my nipples, eyes rolling to the back of my head.

"Fuck girl, how is your pussy this good," he moans. His dick was throbbing, releasing his warm, liquid inside of me. We sat there for a couple of more minutes. I continued to grind on him, his body was flinching. We got up, showered, and retired to bed. The next morning over breakfast we had a long discussion about John and what took place. He expressed he felt some kind of way about me stepping in the way. He thought I was protecting him and still had feelings for him. I reminded him that there was a time and place for everything. "I meant to bring this up too," he paused apparently hesitant about whatever he was about to say. "You need to stop working at that club. I want you to stop and with everything going on it's not safe," he said as he attempted to read my face for a reaction. "For one, I'm not stupid. I know what you do there, I peeped everything the first night. Yeah, you were doing it before we started dealing with each other and even then, I didn't like it, but I wasn't trying to judge you. This nigga knows where you live, work, go to school, and now popping up when you're out. You gotta change that. You an easy target, ma," he proclaimed getting up to clear the dishes.

"I understand, trust me I do," I huffed. Irked at the idea that I must uproot and change my life because of that asshole. "My friends did offer that I could stay with them, so I could look into that and have my stuff in storage until I find somewhere permanent, take a semester off of classes, and look for a decent paying job," I vented out loud. "It's a lot, I'll think about it," I told him, sipping on the green tea he brewed this morning.

"It's a lot, I'll think about it," he repeated mockingly. "What's there to think about? Your life could be at fucking stake, are you missing it?" He pounded his fist on the table as he spoke with base and anger. "You're being too cavalier and nonchalant about all of this, like women not out here dying at the hands of men scorned behind break-ups," he continued. "I understand y'all had a thing and, God rest his soul, a baby together," I glared at him as I stood up to interrupt.

"Don't do that, don't you dare fucking bring my baby into this. He has nothing to do with what that bastard is doing, what we're currently discussing, or me trying to live my life other than as motivation for me to do so. So if you have to make a fucking point do that, but don't try to guilt me by bringing up my deceased baby," I started to storm off, but he grabbed my hand.

"Baby I apologize, I crossed the line," he pleaded, I used my free hand to wipe his hand off me. "I need some air Ezekiel. I'm going to go stay with one of my friends tonight. I can't be here right now." I walked over to the couch to get my bag. "Baby," he called again, and I ignored him, putting on my shoes then walked directly out of the door.

Chapter Six

A few weeks had passed, and I had been bouncing around from Ronnie, Ci-Ci, and K's places until one of the apartments I was eyeing panned out. This week, I had been crashing at Ronni's since we had final exams and it made the most sense for our studying and carpooling.

"You talk to Zeke lately?" We both were getting ourselves together to take our final, final exam for the semester.

"Not this morning," I said plainly, not wanting to talk about him.

"Are you still avoiding him?" She continued, "He's been to the school every day we've had finals trying to talk to you," she reminded me. We headed out the door. She was playing advocate for team Zeke, helping to plead his case and trying to get me to see things from his point of view.

"I miss him, Ronnie," I finally opened up after she finished saying everything she needed to say.

"Then stop being mean and talk to him when you see him up there today," she suggested. We went into the school to take the final. Two hours later, we were done and glad to have completed the semester. Come to find out, this was the last credit course Ronnie needed for graduation so of course celebrating was on the agenda. Unfortunately, today wasn't the day that Zeke showed up and now I'm feeling like my window of opportunity for us to mend things had closed. Why the hell did I have to be so stubborn? He could've easily made his point without bringing up baby John; he had already succeeded in convincing me of his argument, and I could've been less of an ass with the 'I'll think about it' shit. I just don't like being told what to do. I should've been more empathetic when he tried to apologize.

Ronni and I were back at her apartment eating, drinking and looking over her outfit options for the night. She had narrowed it down to a couple of amazing dresses. I had an idea of two dresses out of a few that I could choose from to wear, but I needed to go home for them and everything else I would need.

ding

Zeke: Come over, PLEASE

Me: Okay.

"So... Zeke wants me to come over. I'm about to head over there really quick. I'll let you know when I'm dressed so we can still carpool as planned," I told Ronnie, booking my Lyft. She told me she hoped everything worked out and that she'd see me later. One thirty-minute Lyft ride later, and I was pulling up to Zeke's apartment gathering the courage to face him after the fight and avoiding him for weeks.

"You shouldn't be standing out here all by yourself," Zeke said, clearly reenacting what he said on our first date.

"Well, I wouldn't be if the person I was coming to see knew I was here," I said ad-libbing my line a tad bit. Zeke was standing there holding a red long-stemmed rose just like the first time, he took my hand and guided me into his apartment where he had candles situated to resemble the set up he did at the hotel. He started kissing and undressing me and apologizing for the things he said and the way he handled things as he walked me to the bedroom. I apologized for my part in our falling out as well, and let him know that I knew he didn't mean any harm.

By the time I was fully naked, I was in front of his bed; he tossed me on it and, starting at my lips, kissed down my chin, neck, stomach, and pussy lips. He spread my lips with two of his fingers and began to slowly lick up and down and in circular motions; making out with her, making love to her with his mouth. I grinded with him, fucking his mouth and firmly massaging my nipples between my fingers.

68

"You ready to cum for me?" He asked, inserting two fingers into my vagina. "Yesss," I moaned while my body jerked like I was seizing and having convulsions. As he sped up his tempo, I began to squirt. My body was still shivering even though he had stopped. He was laying on top of me, kissing me and shoving his tongue down my throat.

"Give him to me," I begged in between kisses.

"You want it, baby?" He asked me, teasing me and biting my bottom lip. "Yesss... I want him," I said softly. He gently lifted one of my legs to my chest, and I used one of my hands to hold it up as he teased me slowly with just the head. I used my other hand to rub my clitoris. That only caused me to cum more, and when he felt it, he stuck his dick so far deep inside me that I gasped like he was bringing me back to life. "Aw fuck," I moaned. His body pressed against mine, chest to chest. He had his arm across my leg, pinning it up and was kissing my neck, collar, and shoulder. "Fuck, I love you," I moaned. I was cumming yet again. He raised up, looking my dead in my eyes and told me he loves me too before kissing me then filling me with his nut. He rolled off me. Rolling back on top of him, I stared at him for a minute before I kissed him. I got up and began to dress.

"What's up queen? Why are you leaving?" He asked reaching for his clothes.

"Nothing is wrong babe, I just have to get ready to go celebrate with the group. Ronnie and I took our finals for the semester, and this was her last one for graduation," I told him nearly fully dressed.

"Congratulations, we celebrated two things in here tonight," he said chuckling. I thanked him, told him he was more than welcome to attend, and that I would Lyft home so I could get ready while he got ready.

"I'll meet you at the venue later, I already made plans with Ronnie to ride with her," I said. He got dressed enough to walk me out, kiss me, and see me into the Lyft. Later in my apartment, I was in such a fantastic mood that once I got out of the shower, I was swaying to the music playing on Pandora. I texted Ronni to let her know I was ready and she responded 'on the way.'

crash, thud

My heart jumped out of my chest. The fuck was that?! I reached in my bag and pulled out the Glock .45 that Ronni and I had picked out. I walked through the living room and kitchen; alarms and locks were still in check, nothing seemed out of place. I tiptoed to the bedroom, creeping in when I noticed the window was broken and stuff had been knocked over. As soon as I noticed it, I pressed the emergency button on my phone. Instantly, the phone was knocked out of my hand. I pivoted and tried to take aim at the assailant. Just like the phone, the gun was knocked from my hand and I was met with a sharp, forcefully painful punch to the face. I stumbled and grabbed my face. Trying to regain balance, I leaned on the dresser for support. Crying out in pain, I was met with yet another powerful blow to the stomach causing me to gag.

I made many failed attempts to fight back; pushing, punching, and even scratching. More hits were fired, connecting to my face, chest, and stomach. I fell to the ground; crying, yelling, and screaming from excruciating pain. I could feel the tears or blood or maybe a mixture dripping down my face. Then the kicks began. They were all directed toward my mid-section -- each more agonizing than the last. I was unable to breathe. I was begging, pleading, and praying for mercy. The person bent down over me; as cars passed, the lights from the headlights filled the room and I could make out John's face. SON OF A BITCH. I wasn't going out without a fight, so I swung and he yanked my arm so hard I heard a crack like he had dislocated it. I wailed.

John positioned himself between my legs, unzipped his pants, and pulled out his dick. I started tussling and squirming to get away from him; he lost it, pulling me back to him by my ankles and unleashing another three blows, two to the face and one to my gut. I screamed louder and louder as painful as it was to my chest, but it seemed no one could hear me. I couldn't even hear me and hadn't been able to hear my own screams for a while.

When he leaned over me, I went to punch him with my other fist, but he took my arm and pinned it down then rammed himself inside of me. Tears streamed down my face; I could hear him saying things like 'you know you

71

miss it' and 'don't I feel good to you' each word followed with a vigorous and unpleasant thrust. As he got more comfortable having his way with me, he started loosening his grip on my arm, and I punched him in his face again as hard as physically possible. That only made him hit me again, and then he began to choke me, the last thing I could hear him say as I drifted out is "Where your beloved king at now?"

Chapter Seven

FUCK! I attempt to open my eyes. My eyes are uncomfortably heavy. I can barely even open them. Shit! My fucking chest feels terrible. I attempt to open my eyes again, slightly this time. Oh, God I'm in so much fucking pain. "The good thing is she's stable," that sounds like Ronni. I try to open my eyes again.

"So, what happened when you went to get her?" That's Ci-Ci. Shit. Shit. Shit.

"I opened the door with my spare key since when I texted and called to let her know I was outside she didn't respond. I walked in and the apartment was mostly dark all except for the bathroom light and the music was playing, so I turned it off. Once I did I hear a noise coming from her room, I'm going back there calling her and she's not responding. So, when I get to the room, flick the light on, she's on the floor ass naked and looked brutally fucking beaten with what I guessed was semen on her stomach, not far from the gun and John had just made it out of the window. I picked the gun up rush over to it, lean out and start unloading, I hit him a good two times. When he was out of sight I came back in checked her pulse as I was calling the police and covered her body. After that I called y'all." Ronni told her account of what happened after I passed out. So, that mother fucker was just in there with my body watching me die. I wasn't surprised, just distraught and grossed the fuck out. I try to open my eyes again, a little better. "I didn't even know she was pregnant, did y'all?" Zeke asked. K, Ci-Ci, and Ronni all simultaneously said no. Was pregnant? I didn't even know. A tear began to form and fall from my left eye the only one I could open, the thought of losing another baby. I coughed. "You're woke!" Ci-Ci said, standing at the end of the hospital bed. Ronni was sitting to the side by the window, K was off near a corner and Zeke was right beside me, holding my hand and fighting back tears.

"Good to see you up playa," K said looking relieved.

"Your ass better had woken the hell up soon," Ronni said chuckling and I smiled at her. Ci-Ci stepped out and came back with the nurse.

"Grand rising queen, I love you," Zeke expressed as he kisses my hand.

"I want to get the hell out of here," I told them, my voice breaking and barely audible.

"Sweetheart I think you have to be in here a little while longer, just a little while, until you're better," Ci-Ci said gently. Almost feeling like she was trying to handle me with kids gloves. I hate fucking hospitals and I want to go NOW! Plus, I'm ready to find and kill that son of a bitch.

A few days later and I was finally released to Zeke. He planned for all my clothes to be delivered to his apartment and my furniture put in storage until I was ready to go through it and see what I wanted to keep. He parked in front of the apartment. "I'm not supposed to tell you, but everyone's waiting for you inside, no one is yelling out surprise or anything, but they all wanted to be here to surprise you when you got home. I didn't want you to be overwhelmed," he warned me.

"Thank you," I told him. I wasn't in the mood for a function, but it probably would help keep me distracted and from being depressed. He opened my door and assisted me out of the car. "Hey, I had no idea I was pregnant," I admitted to Zeke.

"We can talk about everything later, you just got out of the hospital. For now, just unwind and enjoy your friends." He said calmly as we walked into the apartment. We all ended up chilling, playing board games, reminiscing, eating, and drinking. A couple of hours passed, and everyone started filing out for the night until it was Ezekiel and I alone. The last time I was here we were apologizing to each other and we found ourselves here apologizing again; about the baby, about him not being the one to see me to and from the apartment and any and everything else in between.

"Did they find him?" I asked, sitting beside him on the leather loveseat.

"No, they haven't yet, but don't worry about that. He'll be taken care of," he assured me, reaching for my face and I flinched. "Did you think I would... baby I just wanted to wipe the tear from your face," he explained solemnly.

"I know, I'm sorry. I'm a little jumpy," I said. He told me I didn't need to explain or apologize, that he knows I just went through a great traumatic ordeal and he would wait whatever time necessary for me to be comfortable again.

Nearly a month later and I was nearing normality. It was late in the evening and I was in the apartment adjusting a few of the pieces I decided to bring out of storage.

ding

Zeke: Come outside.

I locked up the apartment then went outside to meet Zeke. "Get in," he told me, and I did. We pulled up to what looked like an old abandoned construction site with a haunted looking condemned building.

"What's going on here? Is this going to be like one of those surprise dates because right now, I'm horrified," I joked with a hint of seriousness and he just ignored me.

He grabbed my hand then pulled me inside the building. Once inside I could make out a figure appearing to be tied to one of the metal beams in the center. Okay, now he has completely lost it. I attempt to pull away. "Come on," he instructs pulling me further inside. It was John; he was bleeding, burned, severely beaten, had a few gunshot wounds from Ronni, stabs, and slices. Without saying a word Zeke handed me the four-five and as soon as John lifted his head to speak I put one between his eye.

"CODE BLUE, SHE'S CODING!"

No. No. No. No. No. I cannot possibly be still in the hospital. I finally got his ass. I can see him right here in front of me with a fucking bullet hole through his skull.

"CLEAR!"

FUCK! I dropped the gun grabbing my chest. That shit hurt like a bitch.

"CLEAR!"

I dropped to the ground and slowly passed out. I awakened to some bright ass lights and started using my hand to shield them. "Hey, you're woke," an unfamiliar voice said to me. I looked in the direction it came from, my vision finally in focus. "Who the fuck is you and why are you in my room?" I asked him as I pressed the nurse call button.

"Syd, it's me Buddha, your brother," he said looking at me like I was the crazy one. Buddha? Fuck type of name is that. I looked over on the side table to find a phone to call someone, anyone to get the fuck out of here.

"Where's Zeke, Ci-Ci, Ronni, and K?" I asked him, at this point mashing the damn nurse button. The fuck is taking these nurses and doctors so fucking long?

"Who? Are you talking about the characters from that book?" He asked retrieving it from the window seal.

"Book?" I asked puzzled as hell.

"Yeah, book. Your sister, Matia, reads it to you while waiting for you to wake up from recovery." He explained, handing me the book and I skimmed through it realizing everything I experienced was a figment of my subconscious. Damn. After a few more seconds, a nurse finally rushed in excusing herself for the delay explaining how there was another medical emergency happening at the same time and the wing I am in is short staffed. "So, why am I here? How did I end up in the hospital?" I was frustrated that I had no knowledge or clear recollection of what happened.

"According to the police you were apparently run off the road by a drunk driver. They assumed from the direction you were heading and the one on your license you were on your way home, however given your condition they weren't able to confirm it with you," she stated as she moved around the room.

"Your medical charts from when you were admitted reads multiple lacerations from the shards of glass, three broken ribs from the impact of the air bag, a broken left leg that was from what the police gathered was the initial impact of where the other car hit yours, burns on your forearms from what was assumed as your attempt to protect your head and face from the explosion of the airbag, concussion, loss of consciousness, and with everything that transpired so suddenly you went into shock," she finished right before finalizing my vitals and checking my bandages. "Your doctor will be in with you shortly if you have any further questions." She smiled as she left the room. Soon after she left my *brother* got on his phone booking potential guest for his podcast and viewed news clips as well as social media sites for current topics.

"I feel weird asking, but do you remember anything? Anything about that night or beforehand?" He asked wiping his bald head and placing his phone down in his lap. "A detective came pass earlier and left his card, he said because of how the scene looks they're considering the possibility of foul play but couldn't tell me much by it being an ongoing investigation," he said with worry in his eyes and voice even though his face didn't show it. I took a deep sigh as I pinched the bridge of my nose between my eyes trying to remember.

"Honestly all I can remember is two headlights speeding towards me as I ferociously honked my horn and tried to floor my car out of the way." I told him as I looked over at him. Buddha is a bald, bearded, husky, yet muscular type -- almost similar to the more in shape defensive linemen. He is a caramel-complexioned young man sporting an Armani Exchange designer t-shirt, blue jeans, and a pair of retro Jordan's I couldn't quite place since I gave up on brands and labels out of high school. I was over them since it started coming out that they all had some horrific and malicious claims about the conditions of their workers, what their monies contributed to, and whether or not they were racists.

"As far as before the accident, I recall being assigned a new caseload not long before leaving the office. One of the cases I was made first chair on, even though I was already assisting on it as part of a legal team but wasn't allowed certain accesses, I didn't acquire much information as to why the switch... I just knew I had already made all my billable hours for that day and was more than ready to go home. Other than that, I grabbed take-out and wine and was on my way home," I told him as I began recalling the events of the night of the accident.

"Well if you're up to it, I'll place a call to the detective and family to let them know you're up, so they can visit you tomorrow," he said as he packed his things.

"I'm fine with you calling the detective, just give me an extra day before you alert the family. It may be a little overwhelming having them all here at once especially with what the detective said. Not until we know what's going on for sure," I requested hoping he would understand my predicament.

"Yeah of course my love, I'm about to bounce while it's still early so I can have some time to spend with my ladies. Are you going to be okay?" He asked standing along the bedside holding my hand. I shook my head yes, he kissed my forehead and left. Just like that I was sitting there alone with my thoughts, wondering... what terrible thing had I done to someone to be reaping such a life-threatening karma? I was snapped out of my thoughts by a new nurse who came in, introduced herself, showed her hospital ID, and checked my vitals and bandages. As she was moving about, she noticed the book in my lap and raved on how much she enjoyed it and how well it left her in suspense and wanting more. I agreed, noting that the portion of it that was read to me was something -- intentionally leaving out the part where I woke up thinking I was the main character. She left shortly after, and the book was just sitting there. I'm not much of a TV watcher -- nothing but mindless senseless reality shows, propaganda with the fake news and the atrocious violence bestowed upon melanin people by cops. Pass. Hard pass. So, I picked up the book and began reading the earmarked page.

Sin

I stood there shocked, frozen and still aiming the gun at his head. "Come on let me get you out of here," Zeke said as he grabbed the gun from me with a black cloth. He got another identical cloth, wet it from a bottle of water and began wiping my face and hands. I didn't pay much attention to it at first, but he had a duffle bag situated in the room. Alongside it were different serrated knives, a butane torch, a pair of pliers, a large pair of gardening shears, and host of other vastly peculiar instruments I'm suspecting he used for torture -- things I thought I would only ever see in movies. The ride home was eerily silent; I didn't have much to say, just wondering to myself about the man Ezekiel had become after high school and who I had become that I could kill a man in cold blood and not even flinch. I didn't question whether he should've been shot by Ronni, whether he should have endured whatever gruesome techniques he succumbed to by the hands of Zeke, or whether I should have killed him because after robbing me, taunting, along with stalking me, and -- the cherry on a horror-filled, disastrous fucking cake -- raping and beating me, he deserved it all. He deserved a punishment far worse than death; death was too easy. But, am I as much of a monster as him?

I didn't hesitate to kill him. I was almost stricken with bloodlust to have him dead. It was that easy. I am relieved to know and be the one to ensure that his ass is gone, but I feel robbed; truly, utterly unsatisfied that I couldn't see him suffer as I did. I wanted to see him beg for the same mercy I was denied as he clawed away at my soul and mutilated me. Months on end, I lived in darkness and struggled through sleepless nights, laying awake, too frightened to sleep, haunted by nightmares plagued with recurring flashbacks inflicting night sweats, crying fits and tossing and turning.

I guess the bigger picture is that its finally over.

Back at the apartment, Zeke instructed me to strip butt naked as soon as we entered the door. He scurried around the apartment gathering gloves, bleach, trash bags, peroxide, and finally, my clothes and wig. From how composed and fluently he took care of everything, I was certain this wasn't something new for him. He then asked me for every piece of jewelry I was wearing, placed it all in a bowl in that strong-smelling bleach concoction on the marble counter of the bathroom sink and told me carefully wash everything, even my natural hair, in the shower he had running. Without question I did everything I was told. He told me he would be back and not to disturb anything he had tonight. In the shower, while soaking and allowing the downpour of water to cascade my almond complexioned skin before I lathered and washed with vanilla scented black soap, reality set in.

I JUST KILLED SOMEONE.

Tears swelled in my eyes as thoughts of jail flooded my mind, thoughts of my losses and gains, thoughts of Zeke taking me there and allowing me to shoot John. Why would he do that? What did he have to gain? Did he do this to have something to hold over me if things started going left? I rinsed off and within perfect timing because the water was going from hell to lukewarm. I dried off using the long, red, plush towel he left on the counter for me. Then I moisturized, brushed my teeth, and completed the rest of my nightly routine. I was covered by a white sheer robe with the fuzzy collar and sleeves, but underneath, dressed in nude seamless boy shorts and matching bra with a pair of fuzzy white flip-flop slippers.

I went into the living room and took a page out of Zeke's book by lighting a couple of candles, burning white sage, playing high frequency vibrational music and sitting Indian style in the middle of the floor to meditate. This was something Zeke introduced me to during our more recent first date, and after the rape, I fully embraced it. Ronni continued taking me to the gun range -- which gave me back a sense of security after becoming more and more proficient. In all honesty, I felt like a worthless piece of shit, so Ci-Ci and I kept to our hair and nail appointments, which helped with my vanity. K and I proceeded with the "jogging" schedule as well, just to go outside to get fresh air.

They collectively thought it was best I returned to the real world; right after they left that night from welcoming me home from the hospital, I became a shut-in. For two weeks straight, I stayed right in this apartment, mostly in the bed under the covers in the fetal position ignoring calls and visits. I barely ate, too sick to my stomach to hold anything down. I showered three to four times a day trying to wash away the filth, shame, and hatred I felt for myself and when it came to Zeke, I could barely look at him. For the life of me I couldn't understand why he was still sticking around. I thought I was tainted. Then one day, Zeke must have determined enough was enough; he expressed that I was doing more damage to myself than actual healing by laying and sitting around wallowing in my own self-pity. He further expressed that the depression everyone was trying to help me steer clear of, I walked myself directly into by pushing everyone away and the only way pass was through. So, that night he sat me down and everything got aired; I confided with him every tormenting callous detail of the attack. How I pleaded for mercy and praying for salvation, yet no one came and how finally I begged for death. By the time he forced himself on me I was ready and willing to die. I was longing for death's cold, skeletal fingers to release my soul and cast it to the sky.

The more in-depth the conversation went, the colder and tighter his face got and the harder he clenched his fist until finally, fully outraged, he stood knocking the wooden dining chair back onto the floor and landing a massive punch into the drywall causing an extensive hole. Now, come to think about it, it may have been at that very moment that he devised whatever plan he had for John if it wasn't already in motion. If I hadn't been traumatized and paralyzingly frightened out of my mind at his anger, I would've been turned on by his passion, power, and brute force. Realizing he was making me scared, he instinctively calmed down; regaining his composure, he took a knee at my seat, cupped my hands into his, and bowed his head into our palms. When he lifted his head, he looked me in the eyes, and spoke gently and wholeheartedly. Expelling his unconditional love and devotion for me, reminding me of my inner and outer beauty, and promising no matter what is going to come, John is going to get what he deserves and I will feel safe and at peace again. He said for now I just needed to focus on healing and get back to life.

From that day forward, he and I set aside time together for yoga, meditation, and training. Fast forwarding to today where he not only lived up to his promises, he also allowed me the privilege of delivering the fatal blow to the man that held me mentally, physically, and emotionally captive. I inhaled deeply constricting my vaginal muscles tighter and tighter with the more air I took in, then exhaled and released my muscles.

I AM FINALLY FREE.

The gong on my meditation app chimed making me aware that I fulfilled my time. I was so consumed in my own thoughts and emotions that I hadn't even considered what Ezekiel is going through or had been going through. After all, a real relationship takes two people loving, trusting, and compromising for one another; however, it seems that the events in my life have completely taken over. Granted some of these occurrences were out of our control, I don't want to sit idly by while he caters to my every need and be oblivious to the effects that everything has on him as well.

After using the bathroom, I made my way to the bedroom and laid on the king-sized bed under the enormous window practically wall-to-wall width wise, watching the night sky. I was drifting off to sleep until Zeke returned home with loud commotions with the fridge, going through dresser drawers, then heading into the bathroom and getting in the shower. Slowly I resumed dozing off, apparently sleep wasn't on the agenda as it was abruptly interrupted again by Zeke plopping down onto the bed.

"Baby you up?" He asked as he rubbed and squeezed my thighs. I got up, straddled his lap while he sat up and kissed his forehead.

"What's on your mind?" I ask lifting his head with my hand by his chin so we were looking eye to eye.

"A lot ma, but I want to make sure you're good," he inquired.

"I'm fine. Talk to me," I insisted. As I began to massage his shoulders, he planted a kiss on my chest and neck, and I felt his hardening dick jump through the towel he had on.

"Not now Sindel," he said forcefully holding my waist with one hand, circling a finger in the small of my back with the other. The bitch in me wanted to address that Sindel shit and ask who the fuck he was talking to calling me by my government and not one of the pet names I've grown accustomed to hearing.

"Then just listen to what I have to tell you," I tell him. He lets out a deep breath as if preparing himself for what's about to be said. I push him flat on his back, raise up just enough to unwrap the towel from his waist and instead of inserting him right away, I sit on it so my wetness can drip on his dick and I smear my juices along his shaft as I lightly slide up and down. Rocking my hips side to side, rolling them in circular motions, and kissing his lips softly and deeply, I reignited the passion we had been missing. I lifted myself, allowing his dick to stand at attention and slowly attempted working him within.

"Damn," he says before biting his lip and grabbing one of my titties. Wincing as I finally got the entire length of him inside of me, I slowly gyrated. "You okay?" He asks, gently placing his hand on my neck.

"Yes, I just really missed how you feel," I answered then took his hand and kissed his palm before spreading my legs across the length of the bed and using my hands to support my weight on his abdomen as I lifted myself up and down.

"Mmmm shit," I moaned, my body already shaking from cumming. God, I needed this. God, I needed him.

"Fuck girl," he moaned and twitched. I wasn't paying attention to the fact I was digging my nails into him.

"Damn my bad baby," I told him; lifting myself, he tried pulling me back and telling me don't stop. He must've thought I was done because of the comment he made. I wasn't done, not in the least. I spun my body around, putting his head between my legs, and he automatically went to work eating me out and grabbing my titties as I rode his face. I leaned over and began kissing him where I was scratching him down to his dick and took him into my mouth.

"Mmmm," he moaned through a muffle as I sucked up and down while stroking his balls. After I came, I hopped up and planted myself between his legs, kneeling at the edge of the bed and really went to town on him like his dick contained the beauty, youth, and eternal life serum and I had to have every drop. Slurping, deep-throating, gagging, licking from his balls to the head and stroking him up and down with one hand while I rubbed my clitoris with two fingers from the other. I get so fucking turned on when I'm pleasing him, hearing him moan curses like *fuck*, *shit*, and *damn* through stuttered speech as he grips fistfuls of my hair.

"Mmmm fuck baby," he says holding my hair, tight coils of kinky and wild natural hair, then he starts going ham fucking my mouth. I open my jaws as wide as physically possible, a tear and snot ran down my face as his speed and intensity increases with each jab against my uvula. Mine increased on my clitoris as well, and I begin trembling and squirting all over the hardwood floors and his feet. Once I exploded, his fuck session with my mouth subsided and I got up to cleanse my face. When I returned to the room he had his bath towel spread across the wet spot and pillows layered near the edge of the bed. "Come on in and bend over, I'm about to get that ass for this mess you made," he enforced, directing me to and positioning me on the pillows. He placed my hands behind my back, locked me in handcuffs, and propped my legs up off to the sides. Something about what he does to me, the rough and aggressive dominance, turned me on even more causing me to get wetter and wetter with each action. He smacked his dick across my ass two times and slowly glided into my vagina. He started grinding and digging so deeply, rotating his dick while deep inside, colliding against my walls and drilling, mining for my gold. I tried to fuck back and keep myself balanced, forgetting for a split second that I'm currently handcuffed and undergoing 'punishment.'

smack

"Aw God!" I cried out in amazement from the sadistic gratification I felt due to the fury of his blow, the only thing that would have made it better was if he had used a paddle or belt. Being greeted with the might of Zeke's bare hand was still a formidable way to show his position over using a tool or prop. He halted removing the pillows from under me and now had me in a deeply arched doggy style. He slid his dick all the way inside of me then pulled all the way out and back in again causing my pussy to queef. "Stop," I giggled at the sound of the noise resembling a fart, he lifted one of my legs, holding me by my thigh and waist and restarted stroking me. "Aw fuck yesss," my moan muffled by my face and titties being buried in and rubbing against the duvet, I came vigorously on his dick.

"Shit baby," he retorted, his manhood throbbing and pulsating inside of me, ejaculating a warm mist of creamy goodness. He let down my leg and dropped onto the bed and rubbed my butt. I would've loved for us to fall asleep just like that had I not still been handcuffed.

"Um, you mind unlocking these?" I questioned, laughing and raising my arms as high as I could to bring his attention to my restraints. He unlocked them, I nestled alongside him, placing my head on his chest and he wrapped his arm around me to rub my hip, thigh, and ass.

"I missed your little juicy self," he pronounced, laying a kiss on my forehead. In exchange, I kissed his chest and told him I missed him as well. Physically, neither of us had gone anywhere. After what happened, I refrained from performing sexually. I laid there tracing his tattoos, embracing his warmth, listening to the erratic thumping patterns of his heartbeat as it raced until ultimately slowing, becoming steadier, and feeling his chest ascend and descend with each passing breath. The very next morning I woke up to the smells of weed, cleaning supplies, and something sweet mirroring the aroma of maple and brown sugar. I got up, removing the remaining articles of clothing I was wearing that became disheveled due to our long overdue escapade. I was so ready to experience him that I didn't care if he hulked up and tore the materials off me as long as I could have him. I had been fiending. I showered, dressed in sweatpants and a tube top, and cleaned my mess. By the time I made it out to Zeke, he was standing at the stove; smoking, cooking, and nodding his head to beats and rap lyrics. His back muscles were flexing as he moved around looking strong and delicious. Walking up to him, I couldn't resist licking him up his back.

"Whatever you're making smells good, but I'd much rather have you," I whispered wrapping my arms around him, reaching to caress his meat through his Ralph Lauren boxer briefs. He chuckled, clicked off the stove, put the blunt out in the ashtray, turned to me, and kissed me. Engulfing my lips as he backed me into the counters, he kissed down my chin, neck, and cleavage while simultaneously lowering my sweat pants until he was staring directly at my neatly trimmed pussy. I went to step out of my pants and in mid-stride, he grabbed my leg, tossed it across his shoulder and started licking my clitoris like a kitten slurping milk off a dish as I stood there. "Ahhh," I moaned, my eyes rolling to the back of my head, my fingers massaging his locs. He extended his tongue down to my vagina; inserting it, fucking me with it all whilst his nose tickled my clitoris and I grinded in pure delight. My body trembled, I came and lost my balance. My leg was giving out on me.

I grabbed hold of the countertop and he pushed me back to center proceeding to partake in my natural delicacy; I could tell he enjoyed consuming me. He took pride in the insurmountable rapture he witnessed on me as he gifted me with his divine oral talents every time he kneeled to honor me. I could feel my eruption brewing, my body tensing up, clutching my titty, squeezing my nipple and bracing myself.

"Uh un, loosen up," he said looking up at me, our eyes meeting his filled with deviance. "Cum for daddy," he whispers right before diving back in; increasing his tempo, swirling his tongue and thrusting two fingers inside of me.

"Aw God fuck yesss," I managed to scream out in between moaning, humming, and biting my lip. I bit my lip so fucking hard I damn near drew blood. "Fuck," I mumbled as he let my leg down to get up, juices trailing down my inner thigh. He kissed me again, sharing my extract with me.

"Put me in," he enforced, scooping both of my legs up and without hesitation I complied. In doing so, I was quickly rewarded with the slow strokes of his dick massaging against my walls and kisses up my neck and collar. My God I love this man.

"Fuck me baby," I told him, and remaining within, he whisked me over to the couch and flung me across. My face and upper body were down towards the seats, my ass up on the back, one leg helplessly hanging towards the floor, and he stretched the other leg atop the back and cushions. Zeke manhandled me as though I was a ragdoll and my weight and little thickness meant nothing to him. He thrusted his body against mine causing a loud clapping.

"Fuck girl," he moaned squeezing and separating my cheeks, driving his nine inches of vein rippled erected penis vigorously against my vaginal walls. All that I could do, all that I wanted to do, was lay there taking it and enjoying him. A few more pumps and he was unloading his semen into me like he was firing off a clip -- releasing all his energies, pinned up frustrations, and emotions. Freeing a sigh, he kissed and nibbled on my ass, and pulled me upright.

"Thank you, I needed that," I expressed, bending to relieve my foot of the pants that were twisted and shackled around it.

"Mm no, thank you," he countered, towering over me with a powerful dominate aura. He retreated into the kitchen adjusting his dick in his boxer briefs along the way; he washed his hands and performed his formulaic cleaning ritual that had an OCD appearance. Ezekiel is meticulous and methodical; everything about him had a reason, purpose, and a place whether anyone else understood or not. Now that he was in a better mood, I felt it necessary to talk about what went down at the warehouse. For the most part he kept things extremely vague and short which only lead to more questions; he told me to keep checking in with the detective about the progress on arresting John. I found that odd since we both know he's dead and I guess my confused demeanor suggested I didn't understand. He explained that I needed to carry on in the same manner as before so as to not arouse any suspicions, that even an inkling of change in my behavior could cause complications. He said that the reason he's withholding on divulging any further information is because he doesn't want me to be involved with that side of his life and if things did go left and hit the fan he wouldn't want me to slip up and expose anything to the cops or wrong persons unknowingly.

"It just sounds to me like you don't trust me," I spoke after hearing everything, well the gist of everything he needed to say.

"You think trust is the issue after you saw what you saw?!" He asked baffled by my insinuation, scrapping the uneaten and dried up rolled oats into a compost bag.

"I mean then tell me exactly what it is! It sounds like you don't think I'm capable of handling myself or whatever comes our way," I fumed, feeling like he was using what happened to me as the bases of his argument.

"You're missing it, the whole point is for you to not be involved PERIOD. If I didn't fuck with you I'd strap you up and send you to war. My only concern and your only concern should be you finishing school and opening the boutique -- end of discussion," he based, standing there huffing like he was ready to blow down a house. Once the tension deflated, he mentioned he intended to replace the clothes he destroyed by the time I returned home from hanging with the gang. Other than that, it was back to business as usual.

Syd

I sat there poking and prodding at the horrible powdered eggs the hospital is trying to pass as suitable food. In walked a tall, dark complexioned, slender built, bald-headed, mustached and soft eyed man wearing an even softer baby blue button up, black tie, with the same hue of blue swirled designed on it, black slacks, and a pair of soft Italian loafers.

"Good morning Ms. Copeland, your brother left a message that you'd be willing to speak with me today, I'm Detective Thomas," he introduced himself showing his credentials. For a split second his characteristics seemed oddly familiar although I couldn't quite put a finger on where it was I recognized him from or if we had ever met.

"Morning," I greeted him, pushing the jail food aside. "My brother claims there were some details that conjured up the idea that my accident may have been more than just a mere accident," I continued, motioning for him to have a seat in the chair that was conveniently furnished bedside. He began dissecting the evidence as to why it was now being considered attempted murder; he pointed out that the skid marks on the ground were inconsistent with a person trying to avoid a collision and that the car used to run me off the road was later found abandoned and on fire roughly ten miles down the street from where I was hit and apparently the assailant either got away in a second car or had someone on stand-by to pick them up once it was over.

"Anything new going on in your life? I'm fully aware that you're amongst some of the top ranked prosecutors and frequently work pro bono for some charitable organizations usually involving women and children welfare... has anything seemed out of the ordinary with any of your current cases?" He asked, periodically looking up from jotting in his leather notepad.

"The only new thing that comes to mind is this high profiled case I was recently brought in as first chair on when beforehand, I was solely on a need-to-know basis. I was allowed to assist with on non-confidential matters, other than that I have a couple of families on the verge of seeking justice in some domestic abuse and custody cases," I answered, grimacing from the slight pain I experienced from adjusting my position that the morphine drip couldn't eradicate.

"The family welfare cases sound routine, however you being upgraded to first chair then being struck is highly suspect; too coincidental in my book and sticks out the most in terms of motive," he suggested. "What's the case concerning?" He inquired, sitting up and becoming more attentive.

"Unfortunately, I'm not at liberty to disclose the particulars," I informed him and caught a brief look of frustration on his face. "In order to apprehend the suspect, let alone to even narrow down who could be a potential suspect, I need you to relinquish as much information as possible to help further the investigation," he spoke, and an odor of authoritarianism filled the air. He crossed his arms proudly and smugly as if he had just pulled rank and was expecting to hear the verbal tell-all version of a case I hadn't even been able to be fully knowledgeable on. I've been assisting my ass off on for months well before I was made first chair, so to inadvertently give him some information that could get into the wrong hands and delay the trial or have it completely thrown out, I think the fuck not.

"My sincerest apologies, detective, however my hands are tied. Any information on the case that is not accessible through public record is strictly privileged to the personnel on the case. If you feel like that information isn't enough to assist you with doing your job, then file a warrant with my office," I told him nonchalantly and he shot me a glare of irritation and disdain. He wrapped up his visit, asking me if there was anywhere safe I could stay once I was released, something else I wasn't willing to share with him, and informing me that as a courtesy of the MPD they were placing a security detail outside my door for the remainder of my stay. He had finally left, and I was more than overjoyed too because something about him just didn't sit well. Moments passed; doctors and nurses had been in and out doing their routine rounds checking vitals, sutures, and continuously prepping me for my eventual leave. Yet, I still couldn't shake the uneasy feeling the detective left me with; he was too

99

fixated on uncovering what I knew about the case, he claimed to have no knowledge of my missing phone or laptop and I didn't care for the whispers and glances he exchanged with the uniformed officer at the door. Something corrupt was afoot and it wasn't just the million-dollar funded hospital serving rehydrated foods and calling it nutrients.

A week had gone by and I was only a few days shy of my release from the hospital but was more amped and persistent than ever before to bring this case to a close and finding out how deep Detective Thomas had a hand in it -- even if I was hopping around on one leg. I suppose that the detective put the officer up to escorting me from the hospital to find out where I would be staying, and I kindly rejected his offer and relieved him of door duty hours before my discharge, so he'd be long gone by the time my transportation arrived. I decided to find refuge in one of my off the book rental properties I put under one of my aliases and paid for in cash in Upper Marlboro, Maryland. I keep a few places scattered around under different names to house the families whose cases are more volatile than others and don't have anyone to rely on until their cases have closed. I always give the option for them to move out once they're back on their feet, or to continue to rent from me. I sought out the security, protection, and manpower of my long-term best friend Kennon. When he arrived at the townhouse, he had my replacement phone and laptop in tow along with some quick fix meals and other groceries.

"So, what are you thinking, that the detective is working with Apollo and his gang?" Ken asked as he plugged in and hands me my devices.

"Thank you," I acknowledge his kindness and log into my iCloud and Windows accounts, silently praying I remembered to not only save, but also back up my data. I tried to make a habit of backing up my devices whenever I completed an assignment as a fail-safe. I couldn't remember if I had done it or not the night everything happened. "Honestly Ken, it's hard to say; he's either working for Apollo and trying to keep him out of jail or working for someone who's against Apollo and trying his best to put him in there," I responded, feeling a sense of relief, throwing praise hands in the air once all my folders and documents uploaded. THANK GOD.

Before Kennon arrived with my devices, I found some time to go over the physical caseload Ken brought to me earlier on in the day. I discovered that the case I was given to take over is the District of Columbia versus Apollo Sanchez.

"You good sis?" Ken asked, coming from the kitchen, through the dining room and catching me mid celebration. "Actually, I am," I respond, clicking away on the keyboard, replying to e-mails I missed during my brief stint in the hospital.

"That's wild, Apollo has always been known in the streets but never had murder under his hat," Ken enlightens me as he sits on the sofa with a plate of buffalo wings with ranch dressing and a lemonade, sweet tea mix. Even I knew that though, at some point in our youth our paths had crossed. My mother moved around from neighborhood to neighborhood every couple of years. So much that I eventually knew of, befriended, or met dozens of people within my childhood from all different backgrounds and walks of life. Apollo happened to be one. We weren't close friends, just acquainted through the cafeteria and recess during middle school. I knew then he was a bad ass kid and thought that he might grow up to cause trouble, but not to this severity -- then again, I was a kid myself, so it wasn't too much I knew then about crimes, breaking laws, and going to jail. It hurt a little finding out the person I had to prosecute was a little close to home, but my career comes first.

"But do you think he'd try to kill you over some petty drug charges?" Ken managed to get out in between chews, gawking at the Cavaliers versus the Warriors game that was on.

"I don't know, I don't put anything past anyone especially when they realize how much time they're facing. Originally, he was picked up by a uniform officer about a busted tail light, brought in on a possession drug charge after a search of his vehicle, and later tied to the two murders," I told him not entirely sure if he grasped anything I told him since the game cut back from commercial break. Sports didn't truly fascinate me, the only thing I could find any appeal in were the men running up and down the court sweating and catching a glimpse of their dick prints bouncing along with them. Mmmm.

Raised a Redskins fan courtesy of my father and his side of the family, and a self-proclaimed Golden State Warriors fan courtesy of that fine drink of water Stephen Curry... well... just a fan of him and his beautiful wife Ayesha Curry. Now that's a couple I could be a third in.

Before my accident, Apollo's court date was pushed back for two months after accusations of the last prosecutor engaging in jury tampering emerged. They needed to go through a new jury selection process. Once I did get a chance to look at his entire case file, majority of the work done by the previous first chair, I found myself still baffled. Charges from juvenile to date with a B and E, petty larceny, grand theft auto, an assault and battery that coincided with the B and E, and a drug possession charge with an intent to distribute which the charges got dropped for the B and E, larceny and assault and battery because the persons failed to appear to testify. Those were as a minor; he served some time in a juvenile facility before aging out and being transferred to the Feds until twenty-five and DC jail until twenty-seven for the drug charges.

By twenty-eight he started his own apparel and accessory line and opened two auto shops; that information came with his financial records, they wanted to figure out if the businesses were fronted by the drug money or a cover for his drug related activities. Within the last year is when his supposed kingpin status started throughout the streets, allegedly he had his hands back in the drug business. So, either I'm missing the connection to him and the two murders he's being charged with or an ass load of paperwork. Ugh, my head's beginning to hurt.

"With the shit I used to hear he was doing and the shit they're trying to pin on him now, including the incident with you, don't sound right to me," Ken says startling me, jumping up with a bone filled plate and empty cup. He grabbed mine off the end table and headed for the kitchen.

"Actually, I agree with you. I haven't gone over everything so far, I still don't see murderer, but it does raise the question of how he came into the money for not just one but three businesses and supplies. I guess I'll have to wait to be sent the remaining paperwork, which I'll e-mail them in a bit to see what's the hold up, but off what I've read alone they shouldn't have even been able to go in front of a judge because this stuff presently seems circumstantial. I have an appointment to see a judge in chambers to ask for a continuance, so I can get everything I need," I concurred, taking my refilled glass from Ken as he sat down sipping on his drink and belched.

"Well, I don't have any doubts that you'll figure this shit out, don't let it stress you out in the process though," Ken imparted before drifting back into the game once it returned from halftime. He is right, if anyone could figure out, what the hell was going on, it's me. For the remainder of the night after the game ended, Kennon and I watched reruns of Martin, ate, drank, laughed, and I finalized the edits on my closing statements for two other cases. One of the cases involved a woman with two children beaten within an inch of her life left by the children's father after she threatened to leave and take full custody of the children and the other was a young mother chasing behind her no good, older, and drug dealing boyfriend who's in and out of incarceration that she neglects the child for, so the child's grandmother is trying to step in and obtain custody before the child becomes a ward of the state and ends up bounced around in the foster care system. The cases that I come across are real heart wrenching, tear jerkers -- families plagued by drug addicted parents, child abuse, neglect, endangerment, rape, and molestation.

A lot of the women are afraid to do anything for themselves or their children and then there are a few others brainwashed into believing that the violent acts of the man they're having relations with is normal and a sign of love. There is nothing loving or normal about a man berating, belittling, cheating, or beating on a woman; however, the job I've chosen to do with these families isn't to judge or criticize, but to facilitate justice and a haven for those truly wishing to seek it.

A few weeks went by, I'm roughly two or three days shy of having the cast removed and starting physical therapy, yet still unable to put weight on my leg, and both family cases are going exceptionally well.

I couldn't be my usual dramatic self in the courtroom with my pivots, hair flips, facial expressions, and hand gestures when delivering my arguments or my tear dropping, soft-hearted, and sentimental self during my closing remarks. My second chair, Joseph, with his abundance of homosexual flair and grace, did me proud. It isn't like he screams 'I'm gay' to the world, but he reeks of flamboyancy which, for whatever reason, I had been gifted the talent of smelling the sweet feminine odor that released from their pores. If only it worked that well with women, clearly, I could tell if she dressed and behaved with masculinity, however, my preference for women are for the ones who still have their femininity about them and just like other women. Nothing against the doms or butches; I just couldn't get behind the idea of being penetrated by those rubber imitation penises because when I'm ready to give head and swallow a warm load, I can't bring myself to gag on that Ken doll attachment accessory and pretend it nutted. Give me hard dick with the thumping pulse, please!

"So, what did you think Syd?" Joseph asked as he held the large coffee mug with two hands and began blowing on the steaming liquid before sipping

"I wouldn't have been able to do a better job if I was able to do it myself. You were fantastic! Thank you." I complimented him while taking the time to catch up on e-mails and calls I missed during court.

"Thank you," he returned, running his fingers through his naturally kinky hair which was cut and kept in a nice short mohawk. Finally. They finally e-mailed me the remaining e-docs on Apollo as well as notified me they faxed my office the physical copies of the documents. I was getting to my wits end about what the outcome would be, what information had been missing, and why.

"Excuse me... um, Ms. Copeland?" A young boy no more than eleven or twelve approached the table Joseph and I took a break at -- the coffee house a corner away from the courthouse. "Yes, that's me," Joseph and I looked at each other and him briefly and simultaneously. "How can I help you? Is everything okay?" I asked, my eyes closely scanning the young man, the entrance way and the portion of the street I could view from the glass window we were sitting by. I couldn't pinpoint what direction he came from since my attention was fixated on my work before he broke it.

"I was told to bring this to you," Joseph and myself collectively got defensive and on guard as the boy reaches in his pocket pulling out a folded piece of paper and a phone then handing them to me. "He said you'll know who it's from and left instructions on when he'd reach out in there." He finished and began to walk off.

"Hold up, wait," I called after him, trying my hardest to collect these annoying ass crutches and hop to him. Luckily, Joseph had such a long wingspan and grabbed him by the back of his jacket sleeve.

"Who sent you? Who are you? Where are you supposed to be?" I started firing off questions and he interrupted brushing Joseph off him and turning back towards us.

"Look lady, I don't know the guy okay, I was ditching school and he caught me, told me he'd give me a few dollars to run the letter and phone in to you and told me to take my ass to school or he'd turn me in to truancy or personally kick my ass the next time he saw me and that whatever questions you'd have would be answered amongst y'all privately later," he whispered pointing at the letter in my hand that I was crumpling, fumbling with the crutches. "Can I go now?" He asked, shrugging his shoulders. I nodded, Joseph shooed him out the door.

"Well, bitch open it!" Joseph rushed as we took our seats.

> Syd,
>
> That detective is setting me up, I saw and know some things I shouldn't and he's trying to make me go down for it, so he doesn't. I'll tell everything I know ONLY to you and ONLY in person.
>
> Call you at nine,
>
> Pollo

"What is it Syd?" Joseph asked peeping over as he sipped again. "Oh nothing, a note from a secret admirer," I lied. "Just someone saying they've seen me a few times in here and couldn't make it to speak; blah, blah, blah." I proceeded to weave a lie and he gave me side eyes from above the cup.

"Well it's about time you got some play, I was beginning to wonder if you were trying to be an old maiden or a nun." He giggled, choking on the coffee and catching droplets that fell from his mouth to his chin. It wasn't that I didn't trust telling him what was going on, I wasn't completely aware of what was going on or who was involved myself.

"I've just been a little preoccupied with work," I forced myself to say as pleasantly as possible with a smirk and chuckle. "Uh, anyways, deliberations should be just about over we should be making our way back for the ruling... I don't want to hold everyone up with these crutches or I'll go ahead and just see you when you get in." I advised Joseph while hurriedly packing my laptop and folders into the bookbag. I had to switch out from my occasional briefcase or rolling bookbags depending on my attire and how heavy the paperwork for the caseload was to carry. Luckily, so much has started going digital from when I started school, interning, and working in law offices. Don't get me wrong, I'm not old -- I'm barely scraping thirty. It's a constant reminder of how much the world, people, and technology is continuously advancing. An hour later and the judge awarded sole physical and legal custody to the grandmother. The mother in the end, in her own way, did attempt to fight for her child and was awarded supervised visitations. Her mother also asked for her to have mandated therapy and drug test to see her child, as well. Grandma means business and I love it.

Joseph asked me if I would come out for drinks with him to celebrate as we usually did whenever we had the opportunity to work together. This evening I declined, having back to back cases with these families, each one more emotionally draining than the last, I needed a break. My soul hadn't stopped crying for the two children who lost their mother after their father devastatingly beaten her into the hospital where she later lost her life. According to close family and friends of theirs on the news reports, even with police looking for him for the murder of his children's mother, he went hunting down the children at their grandmother's home where they had been staying only to get there and realize they weren't there. After hearing the approaching police sirens, thanks to a neighbor calling in a domestic altercation, he took his own life by shooting himself in the head through his chin. Once police arrived on the scene they found his lifeless corpse outside on the walkway and the grandmother on the floor of her living room under a window. They later reported her being okay, however, she suffered a heart attack after the ordeal and seeing him kill himself on her front porch. Thankfully, the children's aunt stepped in and took them off their grandmother's ailing hands for a while. By the end of it all, the aunt decided to take custody of her niece and nephew and to relocate her mother.

I can't complain about what hell of a week I was having working with these cases when there are people living them, but it hurt like hell knowing the shit was going on. Ken pulled up in a red Dodge Charger with tinted windows and black leather interior. He loaded my crutches in the backseat along with my bookbag, adjusted my seat so I could fit in comfortably, and once he got back in, we pulled off.

"Haven't really been seeing you besides picking you up and dropping you off. You look beat. Like... ew." He said, I could see his reflection in the window frequently peering over examining me.

"Nice car. Is it new?" I shot back sarcastically, he sucked his teeth and laughed. Based on this hot car, it seemed like Kennon had his hands in the street life. Again, I'm not one to judge -- especially after my scholarships, grants, and loans were barely cutting it, he made sure I got through school; and even helped with financing my charity. Unbeknownst to him, well anyone for that matter, he prompted me to set up some discreet high interest yielding savings accounts for him and my nieces and nephews in the event of my untimely death. Back when I told him what I was going to school for he was agitated, telling me I would've better served being a public defender or anything that served on the side of helping people... especially our people. He was right, although at the time I felt what better way to serve our people than to infiltrate the very government that's designed to destroy our people and take it down from within while also guaranteeing that the people responsible of doing anything unjust be held accountable properly. It all sounded good when I tried to rationalize the idea to Kennon. However, things haven't seemed to be going that way.

Ken and I got to the house; after I finished showering and unwinding I joined him in the front room where he was doing his usual of enjoying a sitcom, smoking weed, and eating some flavored wings. I sat in the same armchair across from him on the sofa, propped my itchy casted leg on the ottoman, and stuck the pen through the opening by my knee attempting to scratch. "Pollo reached out, he thinks he's being set up because of something he knows," I pause, scratching and digging more intensely, alleviating myself of the discomfort and Ken looks at me intrigued and disturbed. "He's supposed to call, shortly actually, to set up a meeting... he claims what he needs to tell me can't be said over the phone." I finish, feeling slightly relieved of the itching, looking at him and wondering how things will play out once I tell Ken that Pollo wants to meet with me alone.

"Well, if you believe he may be innocent and want to hear him out, we can go once he calls with the information." Ken agrees, drinks from his tea, places the half full glass back on the table, and returns to the programs. "Well, see, that's the thing. He wants me to meet him alone," I inform him, stammering over my words being nervous and he abruptly interrupts me telling me how there was no way in hell he would allow for me to meet him by myself. For a moment I was stuck on the word 'ALLOW.' Since when did I need to be allowed to do anything or to ask anyone's permissions? He made valid points though, when he spoke on the off chance that Pollo is guilty, is the prime suspect for attempting to kill me already, and could be setting up the perfect opportunity for him to finish the job.

ring

I gave Apollo the nickname Pollo, spanish for chicken, as soon as I learned it in grade school to taunt him after always picking with me during lunch or recess. I tried thinking about that to calm my nerves. I answered it on speaker after starting a voice memo on my iPhone.

"Hello," I answer. "Pollo?" I ask, the line was silent.

"Syd, can you hear me, baby girl?" Pollo asks in a whisper.

"Yes, what's going on?" I asked fishing, hoping he may give some inkling as to what he needed to speak with me about.

"I sent you an address on the southside, can you meet me there in an hour?" He asks, his voice remained unchanged in the low, deep whispers that conjured a slight tingling up my disloyal spine.

"I can, however I won't be alone, I'd feel safer having someone with me and actually I'll send you an address to meet at on the southside." I answered, calling an audible. If Ken was right on the possibility of it being a con, then I'd rather us be in control and have home advantage. As the call ended I ended the recording as well, Ken walked off to get ready and I hopped over to the side table to get my blade, taser, and mace.

"You ready playa?" Ken asks, returning to the front room with my jacket and helping me put it on. "Which location did you give him?" He started for the door.

"Sixth and Mississippi," I tell him as we leave out. On the ride Ken went over some ground rules in case things started going left; he told me different signals, signs, and phrases to watch and listen out for in the off chance something happened to him and I needed to make a quick escape especially in my predisposition. It was a lot to take in, I couldn't fault him wanting to ensure our safety considering how much of a risk it is meeting with Pollo in my current condition. It became surreal when he spoke on the possibility of something happening to him and leaving him behind. I used the remainder of the ride attempting to figure out when and how my life turned into a Tyler Perry drama-thriller movie. My thoughts soon concluded as Ken pulled into a parking spot a house down from the three bedroom, one and a half dwelling that was still undergoing renovations. This property happened to be one of the newest ones I acquired before the unfortunate attempt on my life, which is why it hadn't been given the proper and usual upgrading with wall-to-wall carpeting, granite countertops, stainless steel appliances, tile backsplashes in the kitchen and accent walls in the common areas. Had I not pursued a career in legal I could've made a decent interior designer. Some of the homes I took the liberty of furnishing myself and

114

others who decided to lease from me received vouchers so that they could furnish to their liking. Everything was legally contracted; participants, contractors, and anyone who had a hand in working on or around the properties and with the families had to be heavily vetted and sign non-disclosure agreements. My top priority is ensuring the safety of the women and their families; therefore, I take extensive measures.

We sat there roughly thirty minutes, Ken annoyingly reiterating the game plan for the umpteenth time. "Kennon! I got it okay?!" I said, unsure if I was more frustrated or afraid. Granted and praying all things went well, I still run the risk of being disbarred or fined if word got out.

knock, knock, knock

Ken leapt up, grabbing hold of the gun he had tucked away in the back of his pants and slowly started for the door.

"Wait," I whispered. He turned to me with a look of confusion; I pulled out my phone, started a new recording, and placed it back into my jacket pocket.

"You good?" Ken asks, and I nod my head in confirmation. Ken opens the door allowing Pollo in while checking the outside area for anything or anyone suspicious just before patting Pollo down for weapons. I sat there dazed at how much he had grown, and he had grown a lot.

"What's up?" Pollo asks Ken as they dapped each other up; you know the kind with the handshake, gang signs, and ended with a hug that seemed over the top and excessive. I didn't know if it was weird given the situation or just a sign of respect from the street, but him embracing my suspected attempted murderer was offsetting. Then again who was I to talk when I'm sitting here drooling over him, watching every move he makes, and silently hoping to catch a glimpse of his dick print through his jeans. How could I not find him attractive? He walked in six feet two inches, caramel complexioned, low cut with deep waves, slender and toned. He isn't that bad ass annoying little boy who used to bother me at recess anymore. He is all grown man and I wanted to run my fingers across his neatly trimmed goatee. "Shit, making sure you good before sitting with Syd," Ken answers, locking the door and escorting him into the front room where Ken and I sat in metal black folding chairs with the cushioned seats awaiting his arrival.

Ken remained standing off near the entryway where he wasn't far from the front door and gave him a vantage point to see the front and back doors and into where the meeting is taking place. As Pollo grew closer I couldn't tell what was thumping harder my pussy or my heart; he scooped up the chair and positioned it diagonally in the corner of the middle of the room towards me. "So, what do you want to talk about Apollo?" I started, speaking clearly making sure to announce his name for the recording, yet anxious to find out what all this is even about.

"I shouldn't be speaking with you; one you made an attempt on my life and two you have no opposing counsel present," I said peering into his deep chestnut eyes.

"Sydney, I didn't do that, I wouldn't do that," he spoke sternly in his deep baritone that grabbed me by the panties. "Look, Syd I have no reason to kill you or want you dead, but Detective Thomas would especially if you're not in his pocket and could uncover all of his shady dealings... honestly I'm more concerned with your safety working this case than I am for me going down for these false charges." He said softly, as he spoke I listened to his tone, monitored his body language and looked into his eyes. I couldn't tell if it was the yearning to have him take me out of this chair, undress me, and have his way with me right here and now on this floor or actual sincerity, however, every part of me wants to believe him.

"So what shady dealings is the Detective involved in?" I ask, intrigued, pulling out my pen and notepad. Apollo lowered his head and let out a deep sigh, once he collected himself he told us about the events that transpired the night that caused his arrest. On the night in question Apollo said him and his homeboy from the sandbox, Rico, were setting up a buy from a big time Maryland dealer. Pollo made it clear the only purpose he served in the transaction was as a connect; giving Rico and the dealer a face-to-face, the buy was originally for guns but once they both got there the dealer made a play to get Rico to get in on small arms as well. Rico had the funds and of course considered it saying he was willing to at least look at the merchandise. So, the dealer got on the line with her arms dealer, said he was highly dependable and wouldn't take long to get there. Pollo claimed he stayed to make sure the deals went through smoothly and that everything was kosher. Thirty minutes into the three of them chopping it up and finishing Rico's buy he said they both started to feel uneasy with the wait. The small arms dealer finally walked into the meet as they were becoming antsy and it was none other than... who? Detective Thomas.

His entire story had me on the literal edge of my chair. Pollo continued by telling us that he immediately recognized Thomas from when he used to patrol ward eight during his time as an officer for Seventh District before Thomas could get within earshot; Pollo put Rico up on game and when Sky, the dealer, noticed them whispering and packing up to dip, she asked what was up. Rico in his hast and anger blurted out that he doesn't do business with people in bed with the feds. Apollo went on explaining how of course that set off a chain reaction; Sky flipped feeling insulted and by the time Thomas reached them during the commotion she flat out asked him if he's a pig. While Sky and Thomas exchanged words Pollo said he and Rico attempted to make an exit then the shooting started. Sky pulled her gun on Thomas and instead of shooting him right then and there kept lipping off, Thomas who without hesitation shot her point-blank range before she even knew what hit her and said he and Rico were running, ducking, and shooting. Pollo's voice started cracking when he finished the rest about

118

how Rico yelled to him to go, to leave him behind and started firing off at Thomas. Later, throughout the streets he heard that Rico ended up catching three and by the time first responders made it to the scene, Rico had already bled out. It was evident he was broken up about it; just started saying he should've stayed with him, that he should've talked him out of getting the guns and stuck to the original plan or shouldn't have taken him at all.

"I'm truly sorry about your friend," I said to him in a soft tone reaching for his hand to console him. "I'm sure he was well aware of the risk or wouldn't have told you to leave, so you can't blame yourself," I finished. He nodded his head in agreement. "I hate to ask, but I need you to go into full detail; the clothes, cars, location and any and every small detail even the ones you didn't think were important at the time or when you spoke with your attorney," I informed him and for the minutes to a half an hour, he did. Shortly, after we wrapped up and he left, Ken kept an eye on him to watch him completely leave before we did. I ended the recording almost forgetting I had it going, put up the stationary I had jotting notes, and got myself together with assistance from Ken.

"You think he's innocent?" Ken asks breaking the silence mid-way through the drive back to the Maryland spot. "For the most part he seems genuine. He wasn't even at the scene of the crime when they arrested him on unrelated charges and somehow Thomas managed to find evidence to tie him to it. As far as Thomas I got a weird vibe from him myself during our brief encounter at the hospital," I told him laying back, resting my eyes.

"You didn't mention it before, just that he was there and questioned you," Kennon challenged. "Why didn't you say anything?" Ken asks, seeming almost distrusting.

"Didn't seem important at the time, thought it might've been because of the back-and-forth he and I had," I respond now sitting up, looking at the frowned face Ken is making. "You good?" I ask, sensing that things felt off with him.

He nodded yes, which I suspected was a lie and for the quick couple of minutes left in the ride, we rode in silence. The next few days passed, my cast had been removed having me feeling like a fawn taking first steps and ready to hit the pavement running, figuratively for now, until the physical therapist gave me the okay then I could literally do some running. Every since the sit down with Pollo I couldn't help but think about what we had ourselves tangled up in and exactly how deep Thomas' influence is with that lifestyle. Maybe he was working undercover and Pollo had it wrong, but that wouldn't explain him going in on a sting alone or not having the appropriate back up once things went south. There were too many questions unanswered. Luckily, for me and possibly Apollo the judge granted the continuance. The only question that concerned me currently, why did Ken seem so up in arms about me not telling him about my feelings toward Thomas? Was it of genuine concern or was it him keeping tabs for someone? I don't want to doubt him or put those thoughts in my own head, but it rubbed me the wrong way.

"To be honest, I don't like all this shit going on, you are being mixed up in it and feeling like you're keeping shit from me," Ken started as soon as we entered one of the DC properties after a physical therapy session. "How long we've been knowing each other and now you decide to keep shit from me especially with niggas putting hits out on you, do you think that's fucking smart?" He exploded with pain and anger in his eyes. I don't know what annoyed me more -- that he was so bent out of shape that I didn't tell him about a vibe I had when he knew about the encounter, or the way he was coming at me about it when he could've handled this days ago when it first transpired.

"What I'm confused about is why you're so upset over a vibe when I told you the gist of everything else." I was becoming irate myself, if something was truly going on with him it had to be deeper than this or am I being oblivious to what he's really trying to say.

"You're missing it, if you're going to withhold having a vibe then what else aren't you telling me? I'm listening to every word you speak, like saying you told me the 'gist' of everything. Naw, tell me EVERYTHING I need to know everything I'm getting myself into and you're getting me into!" He spouted, snarling like a great grizzly.

"You know just as much as I know for all I know you could know more than you're telling me given your background. Maybe this coming to me because of you or something you've done." I said and no sooner than the words left my lips did I instantly regret it, I always told

121

myself that no matter what I wouldn't ever throw the shit back up in his face. Yet, deep down within my soul a fire brewed and I felt compelled to ignite his ass a blaze after these accusations like this shit was my fault.

"Fuck is you trying to say sis?" Ken asks, his eyes sharp and the tension high.

"The fuck you think I'm saying? As far as I know you could be behind all this shit, I don't question your dealings like what you're really doing and who you're working for or with and maybe I should've been," I finally admitted. It was the truth, I kept my hands clear and nose free of his business if anything went left and he needed me out here, but that same mentality puts me at a disadvantage because I could end up the fall guy. Once the words were said I could see the outrage and anger that was his demeanor turn into disbelief.

"Respect," the last thing he uttered before storming out of the door, slamming it behind him knocking a frame off the wall which broke once it hit the floor. FUCK! It was rare if ever that Ken and I got into it and this felt bad. It felt callus of me standing there accusing Kennon, of what I hadn't quite figured out myself. None of us knew what was really going on, but it had us wound up tight. I took to the kitchen to get the broom and dustpan to clean up the glass. Afterwards, I poured myself a glass of sweet red wine and buried myself into the paperwork or the case that is driving a wedge between me and my life-long friend. Hmm, that's weird.

ring

The little burner phone Pollo and I used to communicate started going off just as I had stumbled on to something.

ring

"Hey," I answered.

"Hey ma, what you up to?" He asked, in that deep whisper that every time I hear it, it sends chills down my spine. "Doing some work, have you thought of anything else that may be of interest to the case, something you might've forgotten?" I ask wondering what the reasoning behind his call is.

"Honestly, I called to see if you had dinner and if you want to grab something?" He asks sounding flirtatious and who was he kidding asking me about food when us women know men done cracked the code on that being our biggest weakness and that there was no way in hell I was turning food down. "What did you have in mind?" I ask fully intrigued, no longer focused on the work at hand.

"I was thinking you could come over and I could cook for you actually." He said with a chuckle, instantly I forgot about the fact that he could be the prime suspect in my attempted murder investigation, the pending case against him, and that I am the one prosecuting him... and started making plans with him to meet at his place. It didn't take long for me to get cleaned and dressed. I kept my apparel simple yet casual; a pair of gray slacks, a pastel pink colored sleeveless sheer blouse that I left slightly unbuttoned to expose a tad bit of cleavage, and a black camisole underneath with a pair of three-inch black heels which in hindsight seemed like a good idea had I not still had the tiny wobble. He gave me the address during the call and I requested a Lyft there while I gave myself a onceover in the mirror just to make sure this is the outfit I want to wear, that the lace wig I have on is straight and looking fierce, and of course that my titties and ass is looking plump and juicy, which it always is but even I can't resist admiring myself.

During the entire Lyft ride down Suitland Parkway, negative thoughts started flooding my mind on how much of a bad idea this is and what Kennon would have to say about what I was doing. Before I knew it, before I had a chance to text and cancel I was at his home. The Lyft driver pulled into the driveway of the ranch style house, he must've seen the headlights or intuition told him because the burner phone chimed with a message informing 'the front door is open come in'. The closer I grew to the door the more hesitant, nervous, and even a little afraid I became.

"You good ma?" Pollo asks swinging the door open, the savory aromas seeping from his kitchen smacking me in my face more potent than whatever oil he had on that I could barely smell but was also enchanting.

"Yes, I'm fine," I lie standing at the bottom of the three stairs of his doorway as if I was currently attempting to flee like my life depended on it.

"Come in," he stepped down a step, grabbed my hand, and lead me into his home. "I wasn't quite sure what you drink, if you drink so I have a few options chilled from the bar, what's your poison?" He chuckled and smirked as he paused mid-way through his surprisingly well decorated living room.

"Let me see what you selected, see if you have any real taste." I teased, eyeing the photos he had framed on the end tables, the black queen and queen painting on the wall and the eclectic array of books that were on his bookcase.

"You funny," he laughs turning to head into the kitchen. "Make yourself at home," he yells out from the kitchen. Which wasn't necessary since I had already taken the liberty and started going through everything. I had to give it to him though, his house is so warm and inviting. I looked over a couple of the family photos that were visible until stumbling onto an album that was tucked away in a draw under the glass topped cherry wood coffee table.

"I see you've been exploring," Apollo says startling me during my snoop through his belongings.

"Uh yeah, you told me make myself at home and I couldn't resist, my apologies." I told him holding the book to my breast and trying to regain composure and dignity. How embarrassing. He put the bottles of wine and liquor down on the identical cherry wood glass topped dining table, walked towards me, sat down on the black microfabric loveseat, took the book from my hands and started pointing out who each person was in every photo and a memory behind each photo. It was alluring how he told about each cousin, aunt, uncle, and his parents. There was something about the way he laughed when he talked about the fun and trouble he and his cousins got into terrorizing the neighborhood and driving their moms crazy. I could almost feel his heart ache and see the pain in his eyes as he fought back tears while his voice broke speaking on watching his father be brutalized and arrested in front of him during a raid after police and DEA broke in their home and ransacked the place, even more hurt when he revealed losing his mother to her fight to breast cancer while he was serving time. He mentioned it was crushing because he didn't even know she was battling with it while he was young, dumb, and running the streets giving her hell. I just sat there crying softly like a big ass baby with my hand on his shoulder unsure of what to do, so I sat quietly listening to him vent. I watched him sit there with his head lowered, his fingers intertwined all accept his index which were pointed upward and his elbows resting on his knees.

He mentioned his grandmother was the one he talked to when he was trying to figure out why he hadn't heard from his mother and seeing about getting some money. He said it was that call that changed everything, his grandmother was never one to play and told him to get his shit together and come out right or he might as well stay in there an die there like his father was sentenced to do. After that I was no good, I started bawling my eyes out. I knew I was doing that ugly ass cry with the tears and snot. He got up and returned with a box of Kleenex.

"You good ma?" He handed the tissues to me and attempted to help me clean my face with one. "Why... would she... say... such a thing... to you, you, you were... just a kid," I tried to get out through the sobs and sniffles.

"True, but I was a bad ass child and every time they turned around I was into something and she was right," he expresses pulling me into his arms and rubbing up the length of my back.

"She told me my mother wasn't aware of how aggressive the cancer was until it was too late and didn't have the heart to tell me, but she did and unfortunately by then the cancer had taken my mom. Don't be sad though babe she said what she needed to, to kick me in the ass from jail and it worked," he chuckled.

I looked up trying to figure out what he found funny right now as I'm crying. "This not really how I pictured our first date going," he jokes looking down at me.

"Oh, is that what this is, a date?" I ask chuckling a little, coming back down from the intense emotional episode I had just undergone.

"Yeah, a date," he answers wiping the last remnants of tears from my eyes then taking my hand and directing me to the table with black placemats, two that had silverware on them, two long white candles, and a small fish bowl like glass vase that had rose petals floating around inside it as a centerpiece. Outside of the smell of delicious food, I could make out a subtle floral hint that kind of reminded me of lavender. Other than the crying the night had been calming and relaxing. He turned the dial of the wall fixture dimming the lights, lit the candles, went into the kitchen and returned with two plates of brown sugar glazed salmon with garlic roasted miniature red potatoes and sautéed asparagus. As we sat there partaking in the scrumptious food, sipping wine and enjoying tantalizing conversation, it dawned on me it had been an extremely long time since I had been romanced.

It was endearing watching a man in his element, being open, and catering to a woman even under the past and current distress. Men never really wear their heart on their sleeves; they mask their vulnerabilities, pain, hurt, and a lot of time love with a tough exterior. Some were raised to believe showing any signs of emotions besides aggression is a sign of weakness. Yet, being here with him and hearing about his past showed me a side of him I wouldn't have imagined or thought of him from our brief encounter as children or the stories of him on the streets. This raw and unfiltered evening displayed true strength and courage. I appreciated the time spent so much so I hadn't thought much about anything or anyone else, that nagging fear of my impending demise had fled and I just enjoyed myself.

The night had been more than perfect and Apollo, a perfect gentleman. I could choose a simple night like this over a night out in a loud, over crowded restaurant anytime. Once in my Lyft, Apollo kissed the back of my hand, my forehead and waved me off as I was driven away. Back home I felt like a school girl swooning over her crush, my neurons and endorphins had been firing on all cylinders all night. For the remainder of the weekend I spent hours going over my new findings, re-evaluating every piece of information with what felt like a fresh pair of eyes after finally putting it down for a night and silently praying there was something I could do to help him, yet my job is to find every way possible to make the charges stick. Things seemed grim for Apollo anyway, especially with the state appointed attorney he had. I hadn't the pleasure of going up against him before, but if his track record and low success rate of keeping his clients out of jail was any indicator this for me is a definite walk in the park -- which made things more complex after the evening we shared. Then to top it off, out the blue he sends a message that read:

> Although I enjoyed myself I know you still
> have a job to do, but I'm glad I got to see you
> before everything happens.

Not once did he mention the case until that message, it was reassuring to know he understood the brief encounter wouldn't sway my judgement and to know that he didn't do it to compromise my position. The weekend ended, and I was dreading the entire day, well work week period since I no longer could depend on the luxury of Ken chauffeuring me around from place to place. I didn't realize how much he influenced me until I sought his insight and was too stubborn to reach out and how much he impacted my life until reality set in that he wasn't here to do the shit he used to do anymore. "What happened... to your... friend?" Joseph asks as he scarfed down a blueberry muffin he got from Café Anita's, our favorite Black owned café.

"What?" I asked puzzled, barely able to make out what he said.

"You know, your friend that usually drives you around, what happened to him? I noticed you Lyft this morning," he asked, again, fishing. He wasn't wrong, but I didn't like what he was insinuating. At all.

"He decided to take a trip he had postponed during my recovery. Why do you ask?" I counter, my suspicions peaking since Joseph and I didn't talk much on Kennon before outside of the common knowledge that he is my best-friend and he is currently being presumptuous.

"Just weird not seeing him drop you off I suppose, we get to work about the same time and he's usually your driver," he answers sipping his Grande chai tea. "Question, where does he get his cars from? I'm looking to get one myself, you know, tired of relying on Metro or rideshare," he asks and at this point as if it wasn't blatantly obvious at first I know he's fishing, but to what end?

"Rentals," I tell him dryly and redirect the conversation to the cases we had to work on today. It's like he knew I was being evasive and lying to him because as soon as I answered he gave me a 'humph' with side eye.

"So, what happened with your secret admirer?" he asks, again prying into my personal life. For as long as I have known him he had always tried to get me to speak on my home life since he was so forthcoming with his own, but I never felt the urge to divulge any of that with him. I have always been adamant about keeping my private life, private so I don't know whether his knowing that was bothering me or that his being insistent on digging into it bothered me.

"Nothing happened, I gave it a try and it didn't pan out unfortunately," I told him purposely omitting the secret wasn't much of a secret and that I had spent time with someone.

"Your life seems so boring other than catching a drink with me here and there; you're young, successful, and almost as attractive as me with no children... you should be living," he told me unaware of the actual drama I had been wrapped up in. I laughed though, still stuck on him saying I am 'almost as attractive as him', the bitch. I finished out my work day, declined drinks with Joseph who, of course, reminded me of how boring my life is without having drinks with him, and completed another session of therapy. Sitting out at the plaza on a marble stone bench next to an artistically crafted topiary and eating a small bacon turkey ranch sub from the delicatessen from across the walkway from my physical therapist, I noticed an all-black, tinted out Mazda 6 slowly approaching the roundabout. I started wrapping up my sandwich and collecting my belongings as quickly as possible because one thing I know is a tinted slow approaching car is a sure sign of a drive by. The last thing I wanted was to end up like was Ricky off 'Boyz In the Hood' so I was trying my best to get the fuck out of there.

"SYD!" Ken's deep raspy voice yelled out, startling the shit out of me just as I was walking into one of the nearby boutiques. What the fuck was his ass doing scaring the hell out of me like that and what was his ass doing here? I thought it could've been him. Just in case I was wrong, I figured the safest place I could be was in a heavy populated area with a lot of witnesses.

"Nigga! Why the fuck is you driving up on me like that, just scared the shit out of me," I exclaimed walking up to the car clutching the shit out of my laptop bag.

"Man shut your scary ass up and get in," he laughed unlocking the passenger door.

"No, not scary nigga, you know a bunch of wild shit been going on," I snapped hoping to jog his memory that not so long ago someone wanted me dead.

"Facts, but I got some information you're going to want to hear," he informed me as he pulled off from the outlets.

"Yeah, I have a few things I need to put you up to speed on as well," I added placing the laptop bag between my legs on the floor of the car and began adjusting the seats. I tuned the radio presets trying to skip the commercials, looking for any song or debate about celebrity drama gossip to cut the awkwardness I felt. We didn't apologize, we didn't acknowledge the fight; we simply rode silently to the third of the vacant properties which happened to be in Bowie -- not far from Bowie Town Center. Before going in, we stopped off at the local Safeway to grab snacks. After we got in the two bedroom, one and a half bathroom with hardwood floors and washer/dryer combo, Ken put up the food and I walked around spraying a mist of the lavender essential oil to relax.

"Do you still think Apollo might be innocent?" Ken asks as he places bottles of alkaline water in the refrigerator.

"Personally, I do, but my job isn't to prove his innocence and you know this." I answer feeling a little uneasy like this was something even essential oils and a hot soak couldn't rectify.

"Oh, is that right? What if it was me? Would you still feel like it's not your job to prove my innocence or would you do everything possible to do what's right?" He asks pausing from putting walnut chocolate chip cookies in the big glass jar on the granite counter to look at me with a complete seriousness in his face. I couldn't tell if he was questioning me as a person and my sense of morality, or me as a friend and my sense of loyalty and duty.

133

"Are you asking because you're in some sort of trouble, because I have no inkling of what you and Apollo have to do with each other." I retort, getting frustrated. Did he just come back to start shit? He claimed to have information, yet I feel like I'm being prosecuted. "If you honestly, truly felt the need to ask that though then I really don't know what to tell you," I continue then unpack some of the remaining grocery bags with sliced mangoes and pineapples I used for juicing during my sporadic interest in dieting and eating healthy. I started to say something else until I heard Kennon speak.

"I want you to grasp the reality of you possibly sending an innocent man to jail for what could be the remainder of his life all because of some crooked cop setting him up. My point in asking if it were me would it be different was to make you see it for yourself if I was in his place you'd do everything in your power to prove my innocence, not just me though ANYONE. That's just how your heart set up, you might not show it to outsiders, but you care deeply about people. So, I'm trying to figure out how far along the way did you lose that? You convinced me the point of you becoming a prosecutor was to work your way up from the inside and help change the very laws that work against our people, now this shit just a job to you." He lectured, it felt like my own words came back biting me in my ass. Had I lost my way? Had I forgotten who and what I was fighting for?

"The state just wants the case closed and someone behind bars for those two murders and don't give a fuck who they put behind bars to do it and you're helping the

134

problem." Kennon berated, each word cutting like a knife. I hadn't anything to say in my own defense, but what was I supposed to do about it? Quit? They'd just have another prosecutor replace me.

"I don't know what it is you expect me to do Kennon, I feel for him. Trust me I do especially after getting to know him more, but he has come to terms with what he's done at the consequences of his actions," I told him sitting on the barstool of the island in the middle of the kitchen and dining room.

"What are you talking about?" Ken questions, leaning against the fridge with his arms crossed. I went on explaining to him about the evening I met with Apollo and how Joseph was insufferably asking questions about his cars and whereabouts when we had our falling out.

"The fuck is homie on?" He asks angrily, cracking his knuckles and pacing the black glossy tiled floors.

"I think he's prying to build a case against you and using me to get the dirt," I answer becoming irritated at the sound of his sneakers squeaking against the floor and the thought of the scuff marks he's causing. "Would you sit the fuck down, so we can talk about this," I suggest, he mugs me then occupies the barstool on the opposite end of the island.

"I don't feel up to no talking. I want to know what slim up to and why the sudden investment in my dealings," he says pulling out one of his phones and starts placing calls. I ended up walking off and making some calls myself a few to check up on some ongoing cases, the residents at the properties and to some of the contractors for the properties still under development.

The next day rolled in and I carried on like any other day and typically it was with the exception of me accepting one of Joseph's invitations for drinks. I was always told a drunk tongue speaks a sober heart and that was my intentions to allow him to get drunk enough that he revealed his motives, so instead of simply going to happy hour I arranged for us to meet tonight and go bar hopping down Adams Morgan to my own surprise the closer time grew for us to meet the more excited I became about going out and this covert undercover mission I had implemented. The first on our hop is Pitchers, we decided to meet each other there and when I arrived he had already started drinking, slurring, and calling everybody 'BITCH' like it was our names. "BITCH! Oh my God look at your titties, can I touch them?" He asks, without allowing me to answer he grabs them, squeezes them, and smacks the cleavage of my open blue blouse.

"And I thought you were gay?" I joke, laughing at his excitement over titties for a man that likes as much or probably more than me.

"Bitch please, I am still a man and we love titties," he corrected me. I ended up ordering a shot of D'USSE, hoping it didn't end up having me calling any of my exes asking them if they love me, and ordered him another of whatever the hell he was already inhaling. We went from Pitchers to Larry's to Cobalt, each added drink was opening a new level to him. First calling everyone 'BITCH', next was the juicy office gossip, then the juicy tea he spilled that I needed, and finally when I knew it was time for us to Uber Pool home is when his ass turned into Beyoncé in full concert singing damn near everyone of her songs -- even during the ride share -- and telling me how much he loves me and how glad he was that I came out once we dropped him off. All in all, I had an amazing night.

ring, ring, ring

"Hello?" I answer in the kitchen, drinking the green tea with organic honey I made at the beginning of the week.

"I got a problem Syd, I'm not winning that case babe. I mean I didn't think I was winning it at first, but something happened," he paused, the line went silent before disconnecting. FUCK! What the fuck else could be going on? After all that drinking and partying with Joseph, the only thing I could possibly want even more than a hard, throbbing, thick, juicy, melt in my mouth and not in my hands dick is the cold hard wood floors of the front room. Shit felt like what I presume heaven felt like.

One week later and Kennon and I didn't seem to be making much headway on uncovering who was looking into him besides what Joseph told me the night we were drinking, but we were drinking. I thought maybe the defense attorney trying to undermine my credibility by showing my affiliation with a known "ex-criminal" but why would Joseph help the opponent and according to Apollo when I reached back out to him he wasn't hearing much from his attorney. Then I thought maybe Thomas has Joseph in his pockets and is trying to take Kennon out through me, but what's the connection and why try to kill me? If anything, he'd benefit the most from me being alive and well since I'm the one sending Apollo away on the charges that should allegedly be for him.

The trial for Apollo had slowly, but surely crept up on us and of course you could count on me to be late to something so important. It was bad enough I am a part of the team sending him to jail, I had to make him suffer through the agony of awaiting his sentence. From outside of the courtroom I can hear the judge asking for the defense attorney and prosecutor. Although it was a damn shame we both were running late, I did have a moment of inner joy knowing I wasn't alone.

"I'm here your honor," I proclaimed, walking through the big heavy wooden double doors.

"Glad you finally graced us with your presence Ms. Copeland, please take your seat. I will grant ten more minutes for the defense to arrive," Judge Haynes greeted me.

"Actually, your honor, moving forward I would like to recuse myself as prosecutor on this case and readmit myself as a pro bono liaison on behalf of the defense and since the defense attorney is not present I will be standing in as intermittent defense attorney for Mr. Apollo Sanchez and ask that all charges against my client be dropped," I announced.

The whole courtroom was filled with shocked faces and it was so quiet you could hear a pin drop.

www.ingramcontent.com/pod-product-compliance
Lightning Source LLC
Chambersburg PA
CBHW072304130726
47910CB00012B/2435